Dream of the Far North

by
Barbara King

Illustrations by Mary Irwin

Published by
Friends of Peary's Eagle Island
Bailey Island, Maine

Published by
Friends of Peary's Eagle Island
P.O. Box 70
Bailey Island, ME 04003

1st Printing - April 2000
2nd Printing - May 2001
Printed in U.S.A.

Printed by J.S. McCarthy/Letter Systems
Augusta, Maine

*To all brave adventurers who learn to survive
the forces of nature to reach their goals.*

Foreword to the First Printing

In the 1890s and early 1900s people were as fascinated with the idea of getting to the North Pole as we are now with going to Mars. Explorers from many countries were determined to be the first to reach it, but the problems of surviving in the Arctic seemed impossible to solve. Many died in the attempt. This is a fictional account of the challenges for a lonely fifteen-year-old boy, Tom, as he faces the problems and dangers of an Arctic adventure, and develops new goals for his life. It is based on recorded history of the final successful expedition of Robert Edwin Peary and Matthew Henson.

Barbara King

Foreword to the Second Printing

The summer I was fourteen I did in real life much of what Tom does in this dramatically realistic work of historical fiction. We departed from New York, as he does, in a sailing vessel with auxiliary power under the command of Captain Bob Bartlett. We stopped in Newfoundland, at Godhavn in Greenland and at Cape York. I talked to Ootah, as Tom does, sledged with him under the midnight sun, joined in a walrus hunt, and experienced snow storms in August. When we returned home, I wrote an account of that summer and, although we did not go to the Pole, but instead built a monument to my grandfather at Cape York, it reads remarkably like the adventures of Barbara King's Tom. Thus, from personal experience as a youth of about the same age, I can testify to the authenticity of both the facts and the feelings in this great story. If there is a lesson to be drawn here I think it is that success comes with leadership, tenacity, and teamwork. It was more than mere coincidence that the six men who first stood at a Pole of the Earth represented the three great races of humankind.

Edward Peary Stafford, a grandson of Admiral Peary

Eskimo Words

again	a-too' do
again again!	a-too' a-too'
air	si-la
bear	nah'nook
big ship	oo-mi-ak'so-ah
boat (native skin boat)	oo-mi-ak'
boots	ka-miks
cold	ik'kee
come	kai'git
dog	mik'ki
dog harness	ah'nook
dog commands:	
calling	ah-huh'
go	huk
go left	how'eh
go right	a'chook
keep going	ka ka
duck (eider)	mee'tah
earth	nu'na
Eskimo	In'uit
face	kee'na
face (my)	kee'na-gah
fox	ter-i-ang'naq
happy (I am)	si-ma-shung'a
hare	uk'a lek
house (snow)	igd-loo'e-aq
ice	see'ko
iceberg	il-loo-lee'ark
jacket (sealskin)	net'e-heh
knife	sa'vik
knife (mine)	sa'vik-ah
knife (woman's)	oo'loo
lamp (soapstone)	ik'ki-mer
look	tah-koo'
moon	ah-ning-ahn'
musk ox	oo-ming'muk
needle	mer'kut
nose	kling'a
reindeer	tuk'too
sea	ee'maq
seal	poo-is'se
seal (square flippered)	ook'juk
sealskin trousers	na-nook'ees
shirt (bird, feathers inside)	ah'tee
sledge	ka'mu-tok
smoke	poo'yok
stop	ar-ret'it
tent	tu'pik
thanks	koy-en'a
walrus	ah'wik
white man	ka-bloo'na
wife	koo'nah
wind	a-nor'ee
yes	ah'py

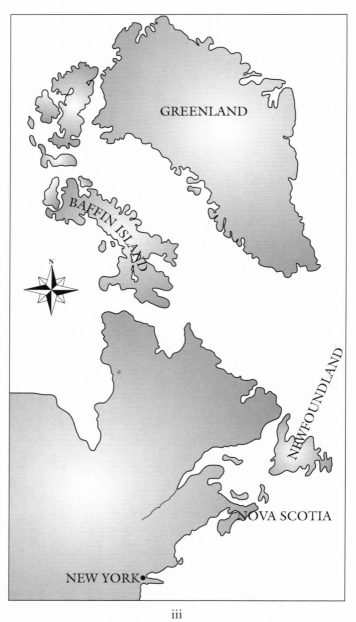

GREENLAND

BAFFIN ISLAND

N

NEWFOUNDLAND

NOVA SCOTIA

NEW YORK•

N

HAWKE HARBOR

STRAIT OF BELLE ISLE

LABRADOR

NEWFOUNDLAND

ST. LAWRENCE

SYDNEY

NEW BRUNSWICK

NOVA SCOTIA

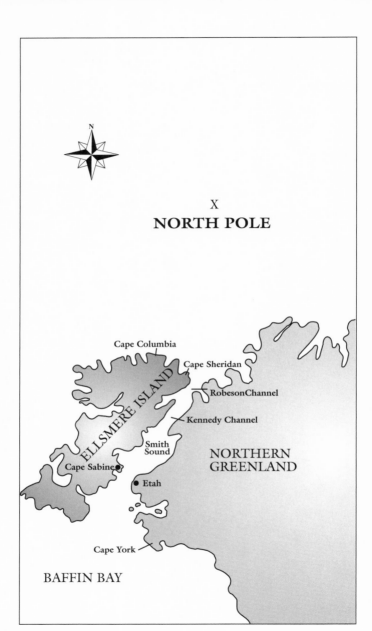

CHAPTER 1

A cold March wind raised swirls of dust as I approached the pier in New York Harbor. When I recognized the three masts and tall black smokestack of the *Roosevelt*, a 184-foot sailing vessel, I hurried toward her. From the bow she looked as solid as a battleship, but from the side she seemed as sleek as a yacht. Workmen were painting the hull a shiny black. When I walked aft, I saw that the stern and its huge 11-foot propeller were newly repaired. I stared in admiration—she looked a lot better than when she had limped back here from the Arctic a year and a half ago.

A familiar muscular figure leaned over the rail and hailed me. "Master Thomas! You've grown— I didn't recognize you at first. How are you, and what brings you here?"

"Hello, Mr. Henson," I called to him. "I thought you might be here. And I wanted to see how the ship looks. She's beautiful."

"Come aboard," he called. "I'm loading and sorting supplies for the Commander."

I quickly climbed up on deck. I had met Matthew Henson, Commander Peary's Negro assistant, when I welcomed my father home from the Arctic on this long-awaited ship, and since then had heard Father tell stories about him. I was eager to talk with the man he praised so highly, who was so skilled at all kinds of jobs, especially mechanical ones. Father had treated him with respect, and I intended to do the same.

Mr. Henson was a strong, handsome man of forty-one, who moved like an athlete. When I shook his hand, he said, "I was so sorry to hear about your father's death. He was a valuable assistant to Mr. Peary, and a good man—everyone liked him."

I looked down, afraid the tears would come, then managed to say, "Father admired you—he said you could fix anything, and that you handled the dog teams as well as the Eskimos."

"Well, Master Thomas, the Commander expects me to do whatever job needs to be done. And I've been at it for a long time." He spoke quietly, looked at me with concern and said, "Your father was so strong. How did he die?"

2

I hesitated, took a deep breath, then replied, "It was an accident—he was trying to stop the iceman's run-away horse. He died of a concussion."

"I'm so sorry," he said. After a pause he asked, "What have you been doing since? Do you have a family?"

"My mother died four years ago of diphtheria. I live with my aunt and work in the shipyard on weekends. But school is boring, and I'd like to find something important to do. I want to get out of New York—I'm hoping for a job at sea."

He nodded and said, "I can understand that. I lost both parents, too, when I was much younger than you. I wanted to be a sailor, so I left the restaurant in Washington, D.C., where I was working and walked to Baltimore."

"Did you find a ship?" I asked.

"Yes, the *Katie Hines*. I was lucky—my Captain not only took me on as cabin boy, but he taught me math and literature and navigation. I sailed all over the world."

"Jupiter! I'd like to do that. How did you meet Mr. Peary?"

"Well, after my captain died, I tried another ship, but some of the crew wouldn't work with a colored man. So I got a job as stock clerk in a clothing store. Mr. Peary came in looking for a sun helmet and a man-servant for his work in Nicaragua—he was a lieutenant then, a civil engineer. He took me with him. Down there I showed him that I could help him in other ways, and I've been with him ever since."

"Were you afraid of going to the Arctic?" I asked.

"No, I had sailed up there. But I had to prove that colored people can survive in the cold—before the first trip a white man bet me that I would lose my toes. I took the bet and won ten dollars." He chuckled at the memory.

I was willing to gamble, too. I thought of Father's dream—to help Robert Edwin Peary get to the North Pole. In 1906 he was one of the assistants who helped transport supplies on the sea ice. He was with the Commander when he made a Farthest North record, but they failed to reach their goal and almost lost their lives.

I was thirteen then. I had almost despaired of seeing Father again, but the ship, badly damaged by ice, finally arrived on Christmas Eve over a year ago. When I saw the battered vessel, it seemed a miracle that he got home, yet he said, "Peary won't give up. We'll try again."

This would be the Commander's fifth attempt. Many explorers had tried to reach the Pole and some had lost their lives, but with all my heart I wanted to do what Father had tried to do. And I was talking to a man who understood that I needed a goal, a challenge.

Taking courage, I asked, "Mr. Henson, is there any chance I could help on this expedition? I'm good with tools, I'm used to the cold—Father took me on a winter trip to Labrador. He even taught me some of the Eskimo language."

"Call me Matt, young man—everyone else does." He paused, frowning, and after a moment he asked, "How old are you, Master Tom?"

"I'll be fifteen this week."

He looked at me intently. "I guess you are aware of the dangers. You'd be risking your life."

"I know. But I need a change."

"I understand. You might get on as cabin boy. Then if you learned to handle the dogs and a sledge, you could be useful around our winter quarters. You look strong. Write to the Commander, and I'll tell him I've met you."

I was so excited I had to take a deep breath; then I said, "Koyenah!"

He smiled. "Don't thank me. The Commander's respect for your father should carry some weight." Then he added, "And it helps to have brown eyes like yours."

"What do you mean?"

"We don't take people with blue eyes—they get snow blind too easily."

I decided he was serious. One obstacle avoided.

"When will you leave?" I asked.

"In July, if all goes well." I made a silent wish to be aboard.

CHAPTER 2

"Now, would you care to look around?" Matt asked. Would I! I had helped build boats at the shipyard last summer, and I was curious to see all sections of this one.

He led the way and showed me the crew's deckhouse, stretching from near the bow to aft of the foremast. The furnishings consisted of two tiers of folding bunks, a stove, a table and seamen's chests for chairs. In contrast to the usual below-deck quarters on most working vessels, it was light and roomy. "There are so many windows," I exclaimed.

"The Commander believes in stretching twilight in the winter as long as possible," Matt explained. "It's dark a long time."

Another deckhouse between the mainmast and the mizzen (the mast closest to the stern) contained the galley, with cabins and mess rooms for the assistants and ship's officers on either side. It was seven feet high inside and stretched clear across the ship.

I was curious to see Commander Peary's quarters and peeked in. The room was large—about ten by sixteen feet. Besides the built-in bunk and wash basin, it contained a desk, wicker chair, chest of drawers, bookcase and, to my surprise, a pianola. A rack of music rolls was screwed to the deck at the end of the room. Next to the cabin was a private bathroom with a tub.

"Jupiter! That's a real stateroom!" I said. Matt's smaller quarters were next to Mr. Peary's and had no luxuries. The ship captain's room was small, too, but light, and like the Commander's had a door opening to the quarterdeck and another to the engine room.

When we went below decks, Matt said, "As you can see, we don't rely on sails as we did on the early vessels. This engine gives us over a thousand horsepower. Three years ago we got through the ice farther north than any ship had gone before."

The gears and pistons fascinated me, but he soon led me forward to see an unusual network of twelve-foot wood beams which strengthened the bow, and the massive timbers bracing the sides every four feet of the ship's length. "Those sides are

30 inches thick," he pointed out.

"I have never seen a ship as strong as this!" I said.

"No, this was especially designed by the Commander."

After our tour I thanked him and took the trolley home. Matt had been kind to tell me he understood my feelings. He had given me hope that I might go on the *Roosevelt*. That would give me a reason to get on with my life.

Memories of Father flooded my mind. For three months after our reunion we had spent a lot of time together, and he promised me a camping trip in Maine. It was ironic that after surviving life in the Arctic, he died in the city. The shock still haunted my dreams. Why did he have to leave me? Now I was alone except for Aunt Bessie. While Father was away, I had lived with her, so I had a home, but no goal. What was I to do if I couldn't go to the Arctic? I knew it to be a desolate area, but some inner wildness like Father's wanted to answer the call of that fearful land.

When I hurried home and stumbled up our back steps, Aunt Bessie was sewing in the living room. She called, "Are you growing too fast for those boots?" Then when she saw my face, she tried to cheer me. "Would you like to have some friends come to celebrate your birthday?"

"No, thanks," I answered, and hurried to my room. I struggled over the wording of my letter to Mr. Peary. After tearing up three attempts, I sealed the fourth and mailed it. Then I couldn't think about anything else.

Ten days dragged by. Finally a letter came from Matt, saying, "Get ready, young man! We leave on the sixth of July. You can help Mr. Percy, the steward. No pay, but he'll feed you!"

My spirits soared. I began to feel alive again. The thought of Father's dream made my heart beat faster—at least I would be part of the expedition. The next day word came from the Commander, who gave his consent. "If you're like your father, you'll be welcomed aboard."

I could hardly believe my good luck. I skipped school and talked to my aunt. She is usually a kind, jolly person, but I knew she would object.

Her eyes widened and her voice was shrill. "No, Tom, I can't let you go! You're too young."

"Not as a cabin boy."

"But to go to the Arctic? I've lost a brother—I

10

don't want to lose you," she cried, grabbing my hand.

"I need to do something, Aunt Bessie. You don't understand!"

She looked puzzled. "There are plenty of things to do."

"No, not here—I need to get away."

"Tom, it's too dangerous!"

"It's my life," I shouted. "I'll risk it any way I want to!" I jumped up, banged the door open with my fist and left the room.

In the morning I was calmer and tried again. I showed her the letter. "Mr. Peary wants me, Aunt Bessie, and I'll learn a lot from the scientists he's taking along—men like Father."

She looked at me as though her head ached and finally said, "I'll think about it." When I returned from the shipyard that night, she gave me a hug and said, "I know you miss your father. You'd be with some fine men—I guess it's a rare opportunity."

The next afternoon she asked, "Will you promise to get your diploma when you come home?" When I promised, she said, "Go to your school principal and explain why you won't be in school next year." Then her voice trembled, as she said, "I'll miss you, Tom."

The four months passed slowly, relieved only when I read more about the Arctic and past expeditions, but finally I had crossed off on the calendar all the weeks before July 5, when I would go aboard. I knew it would be a long, hard journey. The ship must get as far north as possible during the summer. The long winter without sun would be especially difficult—my father's description of it made me dread it. But I knew there was scientific work to be done, and the new assistants must learn how to live in the Arctic like Eskimos and handle the dogs and sledges. I was determined to learn, too, and to become more than a cabin boy. When daylight returned in March, the expedition could start for the Pole.

I packed some summer clothes, my warmest winter ones, bedding, a copy of Dickens' *Bleak House*, my father's pickax and tools, and a compass. At the last moment I threw in my football. I wondered what it would be like to play on the ice and snow.

My aunt promised to take care of my dog, Molly, a big friendly mutt who had never outgrown puppyhood. It always cheered me to play with her, and I would miss that. I wished she could understand that I would come back—she would miss me, too. Aunt Bessie gave me a present to keep until Christmas and a lot of advice about keeping warm and being a good helper for the ship's cook. She even made me set the table, to be sure I knew how to do it properly. She tried to be brave when we said goodbye, but cried again as she reached up to give me a final hug. I promised to write her from Labrador.

On the 5th of July, 1908, I boarded the *Roosevelt*, where she was moored at a pier at the foot of East 23rd Street. My body was tense with excitement. And anxiety, too. I would be the youngest person aboard—would the men like me? Would my job be hard? Would I have a chance to do anything else?

CHAPTER 3

Once aboard, I was glad to see Matt Henson again. He greeted me warmly, but was awfully busy. I met Mr. Charley Percy, the steward and cook—the oldest hand, who had been with Mr. Peary almost as long as Matt. He had thin hair and a black mustache, and was not as tall as I was. He shook my hand heartily. While he showed me where things were in the storeroom, I was relieved to find that he was jolly, kind-hearted and easy-going. "You don't need to work until you get your sea legs on," he told me. "I don't want you spilling soup on my clean floor."

He fed all of us well, and he made *wonderful* bread. "You look a lot like your father," he said, when I noticed him staring at me. "Tall, same lean, strong build, wide shoulders. And big feet, too," he teased. I liked him right away. I resolved to do my job the best I could.

14

When I first saw Commander Peary, I was surprised by his energy. Although his sandy hair was turning gray, his eyebrows and long mustache were still bushy, his shoulders and chest powerful. I knew he was fifty-two years old, but he looked strong. The only sign of weakness was his slide-like stride, the result of losing his toes years ago from freezing. His family and about a hundred guests came aboard to go with us as far as Oyster Bay, Long Island. They kept me busy toting baggage and running errands.

Captain Bartlett was a Newfoundlander—he came from a family of Arctic sailors and navigators. What I noticed about him was his unusually loud voice and red cheeks. He looked young for a ship captain, but he had strong well-developed shoulders.

Early in the morning on July 6th a huge crowd gathered to watch the ship leave. The whole nation was interested in this expedition—America must be the first to get to the Pole. The race with England and other countries had been on for many years. The Captain backed the ship out of its berth into the East River, with a tug chugging alongside, while the crowd shouted and boat whistles blew constantly. As we headed east, I stood behind the guests at the bow, my heart beating as strongly as the engine throbbing below. I had been waiting for this a long time—even though it was an unusually hot day, I was really going to the Arctic!

Dozens of small boats followed us, dipping their flags, tooting horns or blowing whistles, and the Captain responded with shrill blasts. The sun sparkled on the sprays of water from the fireboats, making rainbows in the mist. The noise grew louder as factories blew their whistles and a naval yacht gave us a salute with her gun. For several miles boats stayed with us.

At Oyster Bay, President "Teddy" Roosevelt arrived to wish Commander Peary good fortune. What luck to be able to see him! A huge crowd ashore was welcoming him with cheers and a band—they obviously loved him. After a few minutes he took a launch and climbed aboard. He was shorter than the Commander, not at all formal, and he had a thick mustache and a big smile. He visited Mr. Peary's quarters and the engine room and shook hands with everyone—even me. That was something I would write home about. I heard Captain Bartlett say to him, "It's the North Pole or bust, this time, Mr. President."

The celebration, even though thrilling, seemed endless, and I was impatient to get on our way.

After the President left, a tug took the Peary family and other guests ashore. When we finally steamed out of the harbor, leaving the crowd and boats behind, Matt was the first man aloft. I watched him and the sailors scamper out on the yardarms to unfurl the sails. Like wings of a giant bird they opened, flapped out with a snapping sound, and swelled. The ship shuddered, then rolled forward smoothly; soon we were under way with a southwest wind. What a glorious sight it was to stand in the stern and look aloft at the billowing white sails pulling us north!

I had been a little nervous about meeting the members of the staff, but they made me feel welcome the first day. One of the new assistants seemed a lot younger than the others, and I liked the way he smiled and joked. Mr. Borup was twenty-one, but he acted like a kid and was always laughing. "The name's George," he said, as he shook my hand. He had thick, curly hair, and was very muscular. I learned that he held several athletic records, one in wrestling.

Another tenderfoot, as Mr. Peary called any man who had not been with him before, was Dr. John Goodsell, our surgeon. He had to stoop to enter the galley. For such a giant of a man he spoke softly. He noticed my nervousness and said, "I want you for my friend, young man. Sometimes I need second helpings."

I grinned at him. "I'll remember."

Professor Ross Marvin, a serious-looking man with a thin face, had been on the previous trip. He was six feet tall and getting bald, although otherwise he looked young. He was an instructor in civil engineering at Cornell. He told me his job on this expedition was to study the geography of unknown fjords on the northern coast of Ellesmere Island, where we would be wintering, and report his findings to the National Geographic Society.

Donald MacMillan, another tenderfoot, was a middle-aged professor, a teacher of physical education, French and mathematics at Worcester Academy in Massachusetts. I was a little in awe of him until he talked to me.

"What are your hobbies besides your interest in the Arctic?" he asked.

"I play football, and I like sailing and camping."

He laughed. "Well, you're going to have a sail you'll never forget. And the camping will certainly be primitive."

"I'm ready," I said. "Can't wait to learn how to build an igloo."

"Are you a good student?"

"Well, I do okay. I like science, but there isn't any special subject I'm good at."

"That's not unusual," he said. "Some of my students don't have strong interests, either. Have patience. What you learn on this trip may open some doors and help you decide what you want to do."

I hadn't thought about the expedition in that way, only as an immediate opportunity to have some excitement in my life. Maybe I'd find something interesting to look forward to after this was over.

At New Bedford we took aboard whaleboats to be used as fishing crafts and life boats, and in Casco Bay, Maine, we sailed by many beautiful uninhabited islands to stop at one that had a large building on it. "This is Eagle Island, Mr. Peary's summer home," Mr. Percy explained. "We're getting his dogs and an extra rudder."

The island was heavily wooded—it seemed to me a wonderful place to live. The house had lots of windows. Captain Bartlett called it "the glass house." The sharp end of the rocky island looked like the prow of a ship, and the house sat where a pilot house would be located behind it.

We sailed on to Sydney, Nova Scotia, where we took on coal. While we waited there, George and Mr. MacMillan invited me to move in with them so I wouldn't have to sleep in the crowded crew's quarters. How nice of a real professor to let a boy bunk with him! My stuff didn't take up much room. The shelves were already bulging with their cameras, ammunition, a barometer, books, clothes and collegiate sweaters. Guns and photos decorated the walls, and trunks and a bath tub made from an oil barrel took up floor space. I settled in, and put most everything under my bed or under the mattress.

I decided to call the Professor Mr. Mac—his full name seemed such a mouthful. George called him Don, but that didn't seem right to me. My roommates soon had me laughing, and their humor helped me relax. They were as enthusiastic as I was about taking off on a great new adventure.

CHAPTER 4

I was getting used to the rolling of the ship, so I started helping Mr. Percy serve meals. We had a different menu for each day of the week. Although I wasn't fond of washing dishes and peeling potatoes, being a waiter was fun because the staff joked so much. Part of the time I ran errands for the Commander or took messages to the staff or orders to Matt. He was all over the ship, in the rigging, repacking supplies or carpentering. Everyone went to him for help, and he seemed to be the most popular man aboard.

On one errand I was sent to the engine room. I had wanted to get in there and watch while we were under way. I approached Chief Wardwell, the engineer, a genial giant with white hair. Seeing my curiosity, he invited me to come closer. I felt the power of the great six-foot-long gleaming pistons as they pounded back and forth, their hissing and rhythmic throbbing battering my ears. The Chief pointed out the huge boiler overhead and the valves below. "This slide valve moves the pistons," he shouted. "They turn the flywheel and that turns the propeller. Here, take the throttle."

I jumped at the offer, and soon I was feeling like a real crewman. Before long the bell rang to denote new orders, "Full speed ahead." I looked toward the Chief for permission, and when he nodded, I pushed on the throttle and felt the surge as the ship rushed forward. What a thrill! I'm sure he could tell from my excitement that I was grateful for his sharing so much with me.

My fun was soon interrupted when Charley yelled down to me, "Tom, what are you doing? Where's my can of peas?" I thanked Chief Wardwell and dashed to the storeroom.

I looked forward to seeing icebergs, but when Captain Bartlett headed north through the narrow Belle Isle Straits between Newfoundland and Labrador, we ran into a dense fog.

"They call this 'the graveyard of ships,'" George said with a broad smile, as though he looked forward to an adventure. He teased me a lot.

The fog made us move very slowly—we couldn't

see anything more than five feet away. It was eerie. The ship made progress only by sound, from fog horn to fog horn, her whistle blowing. Even in July there was danger from drifting icebergs, and I waited anxiously for a blow against the hull. I was more fearful when I saw two steamers at anchor, blowing their warning double blasts. They were not willing to go on, but our determined Captain pushed ahead, avoiding bergs just in time or sometimes jolting against the side of one.

Toward dawn a grinding crash woke us. My head bumped against the wall and half the contents of the cabin shelves fell to the floor with a crash. The ship shuddered, but did not stop. George sat up, looked at the clutter and grunted. I wondered what we had hit and rushed out on deck. It didn't make me feel any better to see that the Commander was there, having stayed up all night.

"Just ice," he said. But the hunk of ice the ship had moved away from was as big as a house.

A watchman saw my surprise. "That was just a flea bite. Wait till you see what the *Roosevelt* can do in pack ice. She weighs 614 tons, and she's built to get us through. Her bow is shaped to crush the ice, and her rounded sides amidships help her rise if she's pinched. You'll see how well Captain Bartlett handles her. We're lucky to have him with us again."

I thanked him, and when I went back into the cabin, George asked sleepily, "How come some of this clutter isn't yours?"

"Because my stuff was already on the floor," I joked. "Yours took up all the room on the shelves." I helped him pick up his things. Then I turned my sleeping bag around so my feet would hit the wall next time, instead of my head. I didn't sleep, but the Captain did make the passage through the Straits safely.

In the morning the sun was bright, and I saw a bigger iceberg. I called George out from his bunk. "Come see this monster!"

"Jumping Jehosaphat!" he exclaimed. "That must be fifty feet high." I was glad we had room to go around it. Then I couldn't take my eyes away—caves in it seemed to glow with a blue inner light. It was beautiful. All the newcomers came out to see it, and I watched it a long time.

When we entered Hawke Harbor to take on whale meat, men had hauled a finback up on a slip and were cutting it up. I was fascinated to see a whale so close. After stripping off the blubber in pieces, like peeling an orange, the workmen cut the meat off the bones, then into blocks. Their clothes were soon soaked with blood and oil.

Mr. Percy called to the factory man, "What will

you take?"

"How much have you got?"

When the dickering was done, Mr. Percy bragged, "A whale is worth about a thousand dollars usually. I got an eight-ton one for $480—three cents a pound." I watched as they loaded 17,000 pounds of meat onto our afterdeck—a messy job.

To save hunting time later, the Commander had a supply ship, the *Erik*, loaded with twenty-five tons of whale meat for the dogs we would get in Greenland. He kept her downwind. Later I found out why—we could smell it for miles. Our supply soon became fragrant enough.

We took on tanks of water, and I helped store 550 tons of coal in bags in the hold and on the afterdeck. I didn't have to, but I wanted to get stronger. It was back-breaking work, and coal dust soon filled my lungs.

Mr. Percy rescued me. "I'm going ashore to buy pigs and sheep. Want to come along?"

I certainly did, but soon regretted it—mosquitoes as big as hornets attacked us, and there was no escape from them. I was glad the job didn't take long—I couldn't wait to return to the ship and the sea breeze. When I led two 140-pound pigs aboard, I asked, "Where do we put them?" I knew wood was too valuable to make a pen.

"Let 'em run loose on the deck," he said.

When I untied them, they waddled around every part of the ship, grunting, sticking their noses into everything and leaving messes. They certainly took some of the sailors by surprise. I chased them out of the Commander's cabin and went back ashore to get the sheep. Once aboard, they became frightened, and cowered near the stern rail. The pigs' leaps and squeals and the bleating of the sheep added to all the usual noise and confusion on board—the ship was a madhouse. As I carried coal again, I had to shove animals out of my way continually, and avoid stepping in their filth. Who would have expected the deck of a ship to be like this? I told Mr. Percy, "This is a zoo."

"Just wait," he said. "It will get worse."

As we moved up the coast, about 200 icebergs floated toward us, looking like fleets of sailboats—a grand sight. The water, wind and sun had sculptured them into fantastic shapes, with peaks and caves. One looked something like a bear. Towering 30 or 40 feet over my head, they dwarfed our big ship. If they were this large here in warm weather, what would they would look like farther north in the cold? Water cascaded down their sides and splashed into the sea, making spray that drifted on the wind. As I stared upward I could spot the black caps and blood-red bills of little gulls—Arctic terns—roosting on their peaks. What fun it would be to ride up so high on an iceberg!

My daily chores were not hard. At a fishing station 200 miles north we added cod and salmon to the supplies, and I helped dry them on racks. I was thankful the galley was above deck so I could watch the changing weather and the sea stretching north to where the sky began. Sometimes I helped Matt, but he was constantly interrupted—someone was always calling, "Hey, Matt!" Everyone went to him for advice and he always gave it politely.

To reach the Greenland coast, 1500 miles away, the Captain set a new course toward the northeast. That night Matt invited me to stand watch with him.

CHAPTER 5

Moonlight behind the icebergs made them loom up huge, dark and menacing.

"We don't want to knock the toothpick out of her mouth," Matt said.

"What do you mean?"

"One of those monsters could easily smash the bowsprit."

I had visions of what a collision could do to the bow. It could wreck all our plans.

"You can help me by watching out for growlers," he suggested.

"What's a growler?"

"Boulders of ice hidden under water. You can't see them—you can recognize them by the swish and swirl of the current around them." He pointed to a spot off the beam. "There's one."

Before long I called out, "Growler to starboard!" and the helmsman avoided it in time. I spotted several more huge ones, so they did no damage, and no one's sleep was disturbed.

When we left most of the bergs behind us, Matt asked, "Do you like your job?"

"Oh, yes. This is more fun than living in New York." I asked him if he had any relatives there.

"My wife Lucy is in Harlem. We just got married last September."

"And she let you go?" I asked. I remembered how I felt at being left behind when Father went on the last expedition.

He hesitated. "Yes, but you have to understand that going to the Arctic is an unusual opportunity for a Negro. It's far better than being a stock boy or chauffeur, or even a Pullman porter on cross-country trains." After a pause he said, "I depend on the Commander for my life in the Arctic. I love it."

I could see that it would make him feel more important, too. Matt did more work than anyone else, and better, but in spite of that, the Commander just seemed to expect such loyal service. I had noticed that Matt always addressed him as "Sir."

"The Commander certainly depends on you, and you work so hard for him. Don't you ever complain?" I asked.

"Not to him. I try to do what he wants. He's an

iron man who never gives up, and he pushes us all—often when I'm ready to stop he demands an extra mile or two over the ice. But who can refuse him? He inspires everyone, and to the Eskimos he's their patron. He has given them a lot of things to improve their lives."

"I sure hope this time you get to the Pole."

"Amen to that."

As I watched a huge berg to starboard, it suddenly turned on its side, rocking crazily. I was surprised to see that most of it had been under water.

"Hold on!" Matt said, as the ship began to ride over the waves it made.

When we settled back on an even keel, I said, "I'm glad I wasn't asleep. I bet George hit the wall again."

The watch seemed to pass quickly. In talking to Matt I had forgotten my fear, and had learned more about this man I admired. I was happy to be on the sea, but before long it gave me reasons to fear and respect it.

Three days out from Labrador the Atlantic produced a frightening gale. Mr. Percy and I caught the animals and tied them below. As the ship started to roll in the huge waves, I heard a heavy crash, the sounds of running feet and hoarse shouts. The crew yelled as they tried to grab and lash down anything that was loose. Everything not secured smashed against the deck houses or went over the rail. We tried to help, but I was scared to death of being washed overboard.

"It's a rip snorter! Hang on," Mr. Percy shouted as we cowered in the galley. Tons of sea crashed over the bow and raced in torrents down the length of the ship. One dory was broken into kindling, and the galley floor was covered with six inches of water. I clung to the doorway and didn't dare move.

When the wind let up a little and I finally crept to the cabin, George yelled, "Be careful. The lamp crashed—there's glass everywhere. And the ink spilled and is running around. Holy Smoke! What a mess!"

Everything that had not been tied to a beam was on the floor. After we cleared it, Mr. Mac, bracing himself, hung two pairs of snowshoes from the ceiling as horizontal shelves, saying, "When we roll like this, these will work better than shelves. Get some more string, Tom, and we'll tie things on them and hang things under them." As he spoke, he tied his notebooks on one.

I thought the snowshoe shelves were a clever idea. But I was feeling seasick, and when I ran to the stern rail I discovered most of the crew were sick, too. Matt was one of the few who could keep working. Mr. Percy watched over me while I was abed. I started to call him Charley, as everyone else did. When the wind died and I felt better, I made up for meals I had missed. Charley teased, "Do you have holes in your stomach?"

The nights were getting shorter and lighter—It was hard to get enough sleep. The period of the "Great Day" was coming, when the sun would never drop below the horizon. In daylight in the late evening, I was standing next to Matt when the new member of the crew who had come aboard in Labrador, yelled at him, "Boy, come here and help me move this!"

That surprised me and made me so mad. I felt like punching the sailor—I was bigger than he was. I clenched my fist. "His name is Matt," I snarled.

"Well, look who's a nigger lover," he retorted.

"Never mind, Tom," Matt said, laying a restraining hand on my arm. He walked calmly over to the sailor and helped him. When he came back, he said, "Thanks, Tom, but don't stick your neck out for me. I'm used to it, and there are worse things— where I come from I saw lynchings."

"Where was that?"

"Maryland. We moved to Washington, D.C. to get away from the Ku Klux Klan. They were hanging Negroes."

I had heard of the white-hooded night riders, but it was sobering to meet someone who had seen a lynching. I asked, "Was it better in Washington?"

"Yes, but when my father died I had to earn my living, and it was hard to get jobs. Even when I was a Pullman porter on a southern route I was shot at. Names aren't as dangerous—I just let 'em roll off."

"Don't you ever get angry at white people?"

"Sure, but I remember what my first Captain taught me. 'Use your head, not your fists.' It's good advice."

I thought about that. He could stay calm when he had every right to be angry. I hadn't learned to control my temper. I could understand why he liked his life in the Arctic better than being in New York—the staff and crew all respected him. The incident reminded me of how hard life was for Negroes in the States.

I didn't speak to the rude crew member again. He would learn—he had been sick, so he didn't know Matt yet. And the Captain would straighten him out.

CHAPTER 6

T he gale had been bad enough, but when fog surrounded the ship I hated the thickness of it. I felt unsteady moving about the deck. The dampness soaked into my clothes and made the whale meat smell worse. Thank goodness the *Erik* was behind us. We would meet her in Greenland if not before.

I had time to read—there were plenty of magazines, and I borrowed Mr. Peary's books to learn all I could about the Arctic. I finished *Bleak House* and offered it to Matt, but he said, "That's one of my favorite books."

The Commander distributed 10-gauge Remington shotguns and shells, and Mr. Mac showed me how to load mine. We all looked forward to hunting animals strange to us. Sometimes I played dominoes or checkers with the staff, or enjoyed the music of the sailors. One had an accordion, another a banjo, and Matt had a concertina. Mr. Peary sometimes put Chopin or Victor Herbert songs on his pianola. The day it played my parents' favorite one, *Gypsy Love Song,* I felt the sting of tears behind my eyes and left the room.

Captain Bartlett saw that I was unhappy and invited me to the bridge. To my surprise he said, "Take the wheel and watch the compass." I gasped, but then eagerly took it from the Mate, who stood behind me. I felt pretty proud of myself as I held the course steady. It was glorious—even more exciting than being in the engine room, because that day we were under full sail, and up here I could see the horizon and the waves, and feel the wind in my face.

After a short while the Captain said, "Well done, lad. Now, do you know how to chart a course?"

"No, but I would sure like to learn."

He showed me the present course line he had drawn toward our destination in Greenland. Handing me two short parallel rulers joined by pivoting attachments, he said, "Put the edge of one along the course line, hold it fast, then 'walk' the other toward the picture of a compass at the margin of the chart. Then hold that rule and walk the first." As I did that, the rules remained parallel, moving in inches toward the edge of the chart.

After five moves I could place the edge of one rule through the center of the compass. "It's adjusted to the latitude and longitude of the area," the Captain explained. I wasn't surprised when the end of the rule marked a degree east of northeast— the direction I had just been steering at the wheel! It was exciting to know how that had been determined.

The Captain then picked up a tool with two sharp points like a compass (he called it a divider) and said, "Spread the points open so they match 50 miles on this mileage line. Then measure the distance we are to stay on this course."

I walked the dividers, end over end, and measured 400 miles. Then I reset the dividers for the remaining short distance and checked it on the chart. It read thirty-eight. "438 in all," I announced proudly. How simple it seemed!

"That's right, my boy. Then we set a new course. When we do, perhaps you can get away from your chores and check it," he said.

"I will. I will," I said. The lesson had been fun and easy, but I knew it was only a first step in learning more about navigation. I thanked him and left the bridge reluctantly.

The Commander said I should come to a staff meeting held in the starboard mess room. When we had all gathered, he announced, "We start for the Pole in late February so the sea ice is mostly cemented together, or if there is open water it will freeze over quickly." He told us what precautions to take to live and travel in the cold safely. We all knew our lives depended on following his instructions.

"Until we can build igloos, we'll use tents on land, but not on the sea ice—they can absorb enough moisture during a trip to weigh five hundred pounds. The same with sleeping bags—they become heavy, too, and in case of emergencies they're too hard to get out of in a hurry. We sleep in our fur clothes. On the trail, weight is important. Every nine pounds saved in constant weight—our stoves, tools, lines and other equipment —means another full day's rations for the driver and the dogs."

I hoped to do some travelling on land, so I made notes of all the Commander told the staff. Afterwards George joked, "There goes my stuffed rabbit—excess weight."

During leisure times the staff sat around the table

in the mess room. I sometimes could join them when they gathered to talk over what the Commander described to them. I wished I could try getting the dogs and sledges over wide cracks in the ice, especially by floating over on a cake of ice. But some ways of dealing with open water and storms sounded much scarier than what Father had reported. Once when the ice cracked, Matt had pushed the sledge to safety, but he couldn't save himself. His team mate, Ootah, had pulled him out of the water. I wondered how I would react to such emergencies.

On other days the assistants just relaxed and swapped yarns. "Did you hear the suggestions some cranks have made to the Commander about how to get to the Pole?" Captain Bartlett asked. "Flying machines and automobiles top the list. Most ideas are downright crazy —it's amazing how little the public knows about the Arctic, and they have no idea how big it is. One guy suggested we build a wooden tunnel. Under what? The ice? And where do we get enough wood?"

The men frowned and shook their heads in disbelief.

"Another wanted us to lay a pipeline behind us as we go, to bring hot soup to us from the ship. He was deadly serious." We all laughed heartily.

"Look at this," Doctor Goodsell said. He took a paper from his pack and put it on the table. "It's a blueprint for a tractor house. This motor-driven chain is supposed to revolve over the ice and through the windows of the house. If the tractor gets stuck, there's a balloon attached to the roof that can be filled with hydrogen gas. That raises the house a few feet above the ice." He passed the drawing around.

"Horsefeathers!" George said. "Will it fly over the leads, the open water? And where does it carry fuel? No thanks, I'll take the dogs."

"I heard a suggestion that a submarine could get us there," Mr. Mac said. "And after traveling under the ice it could bore its way to the surface by heating its nose."

"That sounds a little better than the tractor house," Professor Marvin said. The Commander told me he had a letter from an engineer who wants to shoot him to the Pole from a cannon. Can you believe it?"

"Did he suggest how he was to get back?" Mr. Mac asked. "I'll bet he made that up to mock us. Some people aren't behind us after all the failures in the past, but we'll show 'em."

Early one morning the Captain woke me. "Climb up in the Crow's Nest, and you'll be the first to see Greenland. Holler 'Landfall' when you do."

I eagerly scrambled up the mast and clung to my perch as the ship rolled. Looking down, I saw a crew member swabbing the deck and heard him cursing the pigs. Facing east, I prayed the clouds would clear away. Before long, there in the distance I could see the snow-capped mountains of Greenland! I was so excited my first word came out as a croak. Then I shouted, "Landfall! Landfall!" and soon everyone came on deck and ran to the bow. I liked my view from the Crow's Nest so much I stayed there, watching the flocks of birds on the surface of the sea, until Charley called me down.

After another hour we could see that the coastal land was made up of cliffs, fjords and valleys. Rising vertically out of the sea, the 2500-foot cliffs looked like dams holding back the inland ice and snow. Below them, blue and white bergs of many shapes gleamed in the sun. What a spectacular land! I could hardly believe I was seeing this part of the world, so strange to me.

Near shore I saw seals sunning on floes, and many kinds of birds flew about the ship. Some were like gulls—white, with black legs, and the tips of their gray wings looked as if they had been dipped in black ink. Their cries sounded mournful. Professor Marvin said they were called kittiwakes.

Charley had kept me busy when the Captain changed course, but I would find time to visit the bridge later. The Captain squeezed his way between the cliffs and the floating bergs, scraping against some of them. The constant jolting and bumping made it hard to walk the deck, and I couldn't help spilling things on Charley's clean floor.

CHAPTER 7

The shore was different from any I had seen before. In the valleys between the cliffs, the ends of glaciers jutted out into the water, ninety to a hundred feet high, with caves and fissures in them. What scenery! As I watched from the rail one day, a section of the end of one cracked from its weight with a loud retort and fell into the water.

"The birth of an iceberg," Professor Marvin commented.

"How can solid ice move?" I asked.

"I believe the weight is so great that the pressure of it melts the bottom. Then gravity takes over, and it slides down."

"How fast?"

"We don't know—maybe sixty to eighty feet a day." If that were so, I hoped to see the end of another one crack soon, but I certainly didn't expect what the next one would be like.

On July 27th, the Captain blew the boat whistle and rang the bells. That brought everyone out on deck—the ship was crossing the Arctic Circle. Charley joked, "That bump we went over woke me up."

The nights were no longer dark at all—the sun never dropped below the horizon, but circled around the sky all night, from the south in the morning to the north at night. I could tell day from night only by the clock, and it was hard to sleep.

At the Danish settlement at Godhavn, Mr. Peary and the staff went ashore in the evening and stayed until morning. The Mate took the ship far up the bay to anchor it near where he wanted to go ashore. I didn't welcome what happened to me early in the morning. Alone in the galley, I heard a sound like thunder echoing around the mountains. It kept up for two minutes, while I waited anxiously for it to stop. Then someone hollered, "The whole front of the glacier just fell off! Tidal wave coming!"

I didn't know what to do, and I was so scared I couldn't move. The next second I saw a 20-foot wall of water rushing toward the bow of the ship. I gasped and scrambled toward the mizzenmast, wrapped my arms around it, and locked my fingers.

"Hang on!" the Mate called. Even the storm

out at sea was not as frightening as this. The next thing I knew, the bow pointed to the sky at a forty-five degree angle. Salt water hit my face, and my feet slipped out from under me. I was so terrified I screamed. My arms and fingers stretched with the pull on them. I heard loud thumps of objects hitting the deck houses.

When the wave passed, the ship rocked, making several deep bows toward the shore. A few smaller waves followed; then I stopped shaking. I was drenched, but alive and not battered. When I looked around, the sea behind us was full of floating articles, and the crew lowered a boat to collect them before they sank. I was certain some were already on the bottom. Charley came looking for me. "Thank heaven you're still aboard. Are you hurt?"

I told him, "No, I'm all right, but I've never been so scared. I thought tidal waves happened in Australia—I didn't expect one in the Arctic."

Nor did I expect to be faced with the work that was ahead of me. The galley floor was littered with broken dishes and bent pots. It took me hours to clean up and put away what was still usable, but it was good to be in calm water again. I could hear the pigs squealing down in the hold, where Charley was sorting out a jumbled mess in the store-

room. Lucky the animals hadn't been on deck—
they would have gone overboard.

In the morning we welcomed the Commander
and party back aboard at Godhavn, and told them
what they had escaped. Then we sailed on toward
Cape York, arriving there on August 1st. Near the
rocky headland a gigantic glacier rose to the dis-
tant ice cap; to the north I saw barren red-brown
hills and sandstone cliffs. On the shore were the
tents of the first of Eskimo settlements we would
see. We were 840 miles from the Pole.

As the ship approached the village, the *Roosevelt*
let out a loud toot, and soon Eskimos were jumping up and down on the shore and waving to welcome us. I could hardly wait to get a closer look.
When the ship was anchored, the crew lowered a
whaleboat. As soon as Peary and Matt landed, the
Eskimos helped pull the boat ashore and surrounded them, all wanting attention. Charley trans-
lated what they were shouting: "Mahri Pahluk!"
(Dear Matthew) "Illitarnanek Pearyaksoah!" (Glad
to see you, Big Peary). I was surprised by the Eskimos' show of affection toward them.

It wasn't long before some came aboard—most
were plump and short, and all had long black
tangled hair. They were bronze-skinned, with
smooth, round faces and small, wide noses. Their

clothes and boots were made from sealskin. They were all very friendly, with faces that beamed at me, showing strong white teeth when they grinned. Right away I noticed their strong smell.

Charley explained, "It's their diet of meat and blubber and the fact that they don't wash. Even if they wanted to, they wouldn't have oil enough to heat water for baths. At least they strip naked in their houses and dry their clothes."

Though they weren't clean, they were good-natured, and looked curiously at everything around them. Charley and I invited them into the mess-room and gave them hot coffee, but those who hadn't had it before, didn't like it. A few had learned to enjoy it when Charley was there two years ago.

After a month at sea, I couldn't wait to go ashore. Soon I had my chance. The gravel under foot was bare of snow. I staggered for a while on my sea legs; then I walked up the valley behind the tents where dwarf willows grew beside a stream, and soft, beautiful moss—some with pink flowers—lined its banks. Patches of bright buttercups and yellow poppies bloomed nearby. Plump lemmings, little mouse-like rodents, scurried all around me, and I admired their summer "pepper and salt" suits of white-tipped rusty-brown hairs. Some clicked their teeth and pawed the air with their front feet. What a nice pet one would be! But they were too quick to catch. I was sorry when Charley called me back aboard.

Matt was already trading knives, wood and tools for dogs, skins, and ropes made from sealskin. He also had to help se-lect which Eskimos would join the expe-dition.

"I know the men we want," he told us. "They think be-ing on the *Roosevelt* will be easy living— they won't starve. But most won't go out on the sea ice. They have never had any reason to—they can't hunt there and they are afraid of it."

I knew one reason for their fear. Father had told me that when Mr. Peary and three Eskimos were returning on the last trip, they were delayed by the Big Lead, a mile-wide stretch of open water. They had run out of food and fuel waiting for it to freeze over. The ice had drifted east; they finally landed in Greenland and found musk oxen, which saved their lives.

CHAPTER 8

The trading at Cape York was soon completed, and the *Roosevelt* set sail for Etah, over 100 miles north, where we would get most of our Eskimo helpers and dogs, and a large supply of fresh meat. It took my breath away to see the sea alive with icebergs, some cemented together with pack ice. Up there they were *big*, some 200 feet high, a mile long and square or oblong—the sun hadn't changed their shapes yet. Captain Bartlett fielded the bay like a halfback, picking his way between the bergs and the rock walls on shore.

A short time later, when I was mixing dough in the galley, I looked out and couldn't believe my eyes. The permanent snow above the cliffs was red! It looked like blood. I dashed out on deck and yelled to George. He and the other assistants came to the rail. We all stared at it in disbelief.

"How can that be?" I asked Professor Marvin.

"I've read about that," he said. "The English named them the Crimson Cliffs. The color is caused by protoplasm cells, living on just snow and air." I would never forget that sight. This was a strange and beautiful land, with a surprise on every day of our journey. It was odd to be watching snow and icebergs while the temperature was fifty degrees.

Farther north I could see a glow in the sky. Mr. Marvin explained, "That's an 'ice blink.' A domed ice cap covers northern Greenland and fills in the valleys between mountains. The sun reflects the whiteness of it against the sky."

At Whale Sound I was surprised to see white whales swimming near us. They had no dorsal fins, and they slid so smoothly into a dive their huge tails hardly rippled the water.

"I think they are playing," George said. "And they're not afraid of us." They stayed in sight for almost an hour—I was glad I didn't have a chore right then so I could watch them.

On August 12th we arrived at Etah. Cliffs, waterfalls, and a white dome of snow and ice rose behind the village of tents. Men in kayaks came out to meet us, and a huge group of shouting Eskimos gathered to greet Matt and the Commander when they landed.

Charley and I helped haul equipment to the rail to be taken ashore. Matt soon began to select more Eskimos he and Mr. Peary wanted to take north. At dinner he reported, "In spite of their close call on the last trip, Ootah, Egingwah and his brother, Seegloo, are going with us again."

"After almost losing their lives on the last trip?" I asked.

"Yes, they look up to the Commander—he's their patron, and they badly need the rewards he gives them."

"What about their families?"

"Oh, they travel with them. The men depend on their wives to sew, and tend the lamps and their wet clothes. The Commander needs them for sewing our new furs and mending old ones, as well as for hunting and other chores. They work as hard as the men."

When I had time to go ashore the men were friendly and let me approach their dogs. I didn't touch them, though—I wasn't anxious to feel their sharp teeth. Many were gray or black, some white with spots of color; most had mixed colors. The hairs of their outer coats were stiff, but I knew that underneath was a layer of fine hair, thick enough

to keep the skin dry. They didn't look like Molly—
they were heavier, their ears stood up and their
bushy tails curled over their backs. The males
weighed almost a hundred pounds; the females
were smaller. They all had broad chests and powerful legs, and their paws were large and hairy, protected by thick pads. I hoped I could learn to drive
a team.

Some of the families were going aboard, and I
followed them. They huddled on top of the deck
houses, and started teaching the white men the
Eskimo language, with Matt as interpreter. I was
amazed at how complicated it is. I hadn't expected
that—I thought it would be easy to learn because
there are fewer things to name than at home.

Words described a seal doing different things—
such as drifting on an ice floe, blowing, or coming
out of the water. I had to learn fifteen different
ones for a seal, but each word would take many in
English to explain it. Counting to five was easy—
atasuk, magluk, pingersut, sissami, tedlumat; but
six was "second hand, first finger"—igluana atasuk.

Our teachers all laughed at me and the staff members. It was so frustrating. When we got it right, they
cheered. But it made me humble to hear one of the
older Eskimos saying to Mr. Peary in perfect English:
"Like the sun you always come back."

Our guests were very sociable—I often heard their excited chatter and merry laughter. They were also willing helpers—sometimes too willing, getting in my way in the galley day and night, eating at odd hours. Matt continually chased them out of his quarters, but they were not offended.

Mr. Peary told the staff, "They are like children in some ways and you will have to learn to manage them." He tolerated their curiosity and pranks because he had learned so much from them and needed their labor as dog handlers, sledge drivers and hunters. He knew the whole tribe, and was firm with them, but generous, too, getting what he wanted without using fear or threats.

Seegloo received a Springfield rifle and a Winchester for his pack of dogs, and to persuade the reluctant families to join him, the Commander offered tools, knives, wood, harpoon shafts and rifles. This time he promised unusual gifts of a whaleboat and a tent to those who would be chosen to go all the way to the Pole—unheard of wealth in the eyes of a native.

Ooqueah (pronounced Oo-qwee-a), only nineteen, the youngest of the Eskimo men, hoped to be one of those few. If he went to the Pole he would finally have enough possessions to set up his own household and take the beautiful young Minaq for his wife.

The crew lived in the starboard half of the forward deck house, and the Eskimos settled on the port side. The Commander ordered Matt to build some platforms for them outside and above the deck, and make curtained rooms. "Families should have private sleeping quarters and a place to do their own cooking," he said. "And give them some pots and utensils."

Charley cooked beans, hash and other things from the ship's stores for them. They tried everything and seemed to enjoy it all. "They're used to surviving only on meat, blood and blubber," Charley said. I had trouble imagining that.

It was Mr. Peary's rule that the members of the crew take a bath once a week. Ooqueah wanted to try it, too. I found him bare to the waist in the galley, preparing to scrub himself from a soup pot.

Charley yelled, "Arretit! (Stop!) I need that water and pot for cooking."

The Eskimo smiled and gave the pot of water back. I liked him—I gave him some soap and promised to get him some hot water later. He said, "Thank you" in English, but his surprise and wide grin had already thanked me.

Ooqueah was full of pranks and laughed at some of my habits—he was especially amused and curious when I used my toothbrush. "Why?" he asked. I tried to explain, but he didn't know what a germ was.

He loved to mimic my actions. When one of the pigs ran in front of me, I tripped and fell, twisting my wrist. I cried, "Aahh! Blast it!" I was so mad at the pig I tried to kick it, but it escaped. I kicked a barrel instead.

Ooqueah laughed at me, kicked the barrel and shouted, "Aahh! Blast it!" I couldn't help laughing, too.

He showed me his favorite game, Arsaarartuq—finger pulling. We stood side by side, facing the same way, and each of us put an arm behind the head of the other. He put a finger in my mouth, over my lower teeth, and I reached for his jaw. We were both supposed to pull until one quit. I was tempted to bite his finger and it didn't take long for me to give in. Then we pulled interlocked fingers. He was so strong I decided to avoid that game—I wanted to keep my hands steady for serving meals.

I liked another contest better—we sat on the floor facing each other, clasping our hands. He braced his feet against mine, and we pulled to see who could pull the other from his seat onto his feet, without getting up. I showed that one to George, who won easily. I was as big as he, but he was stronger.

Each day I learned more about my fascinating new friends. They called themselves Inuit (the people). We called them Eskimos (those who eat raw meat), and to them we were Kabloonas (white men). The women with babies carried them on their backs in a pouch under their kooletahs. Since the infants were naked and were held close to the mother's skin to keep warm, I couldn't help imagining what else they did on their mothers' backs.

I was surprised at how quickly the men and women learned to use new tools. And even though they desperately needed ours, they didn't steal them. They seemed so happy—they and their children laughed more than we did. And they were not as selfish as white people; all members of the tribe shared whatever they had. I noticed that although they often heard the crew stretch the truth, they didn't lie. When I told Ooqueah about the new elevated trains in New York City he didn't believe me and said, "It's no good to lie." I had to get Matt to tell him what I said was true.

I learned from Ooqueah that he believed the dangers he would face were caused by Tornarsuk, an evil spirit. But Matt had persuaded him and others that the United States Navy was a more powerful force. Hadn't it protected Mr. Peary through all the dangers and brought him safely back? I realized that Matt's influence with the Eskimos was an important factor in the success of the expedition.

CHAPTER 9

One morning I joined Mr. Mac and George to look for geese on a nearby island. We approached a bay where a flock was feeding. Thinking I had a goose in my sights, I fired. To my surprise the bird didn't move. I tried again—no luck. The others were having trouble, too, and George yelled, "Horsefeathers! They're farther away than they seem!"

Finally we realized that in the clear air with no trees or any shadows, we couldn't judge distances. I then learned to wait until I was right on top of my target before I fired. Still, a goose I shot would be thirty yards off. By the end of the day, however, we returned in triumph to the ship with dozens of geese and ducks. But when I had to spend hours plucking them and preparing them for roasting, or to boil for soup, my high spirits disappeared.

Every evening I heard a strange chattering sound in the distance, which grew loud as thousands of birds flew in from the sea in a stream toward the mountainside. They were the size of starlings, black above and white underneath, with very short stubby bills. The size of the flock and the noise they made were unbelievable. One day at suppertime I looked toward the perpendicular cliffs and could see the tiny figures of Eskimos. "What are they doing up there?" I asked Charley.

"The little auks nest on narrow ledges. They're catching them."

"How?"

"In nets at the end of fifteen-foot poles. They mount the nets on hoops about two feet in diameter."

"How do the men get up there?"

"They climb to the plateau above; then a man on the top lowers another by sealskin lines. Go on ashore and watch them, but don't go out of sight—I might need you."

Behind the tents a cascade of melted snow tumbled down from the cliffs. I walked closer to watch the men on the ledges leaning out and swinging the nets. They were taking a big risk to gather food. What must it be like to have to work so hard to eat? What a difference from the way we hunt! I returned to the ship, thinking how courageously these people had adjusted to a hard life. I learned another use of the auks when Matt proudly showed me his shirt. "It took 160 bird skins for Ahnalka's wife to make it," he said.

In a rare time of leisure, Matt planned to visit Ahnalka. He urged me to go with him, and I gladly agreed. The deerskin tent was close to the shore, held up by one pole in the center, the sides anchored by rocks.

"Sainak sunai," Matt said in greeting, "a pleasure, and happy to be here."

"Assukiak," Ahnalka answered. "The same with us."

He and his friend Ikwah welcomed me with smiles, and Ahnalka helped me take off my jacket. The tent was warm inside—everyone was bare to the waist, including Ahnalka's wife. I blushed and tried not to stare. To hide my red face, I took off my shirt. The mother licked her baby, washing it like a cat with a kitten. One child was rubbing dirt from his face with a bird skin. Another played with toys carved from ivory.

I sat squeezed between Matt and the men. Seal oil lamps with wicks of dried moss glowed on the ground. Others were used for warming water in soapstone pots. The seal and walrus meat offered were only heated, not cooked. Ahnalka bit the edge of a hunk of meat and used his knife to cut off a piece. I tried it, but since my nose isn't as small as his, this seemed like a risky method of getting a bite.

A special kind of food was served. A small sealskin sack had been brought in, and I could smell the contents—it wasn't appetizing. Birds netted in the spring had been stored in the sack and softened by soaking in oil. I watched Ahnalka pull the feathers from the little auk and skin it. It looked rotten. He handed some around, and I busied myself pretending to retie my boot while it went by. The smell was overpowering. What a menu! How could they stand having only meat to eat? I was really thankful for Charley's cooking.

After the meal, the men sang, swinging their heads from side to side. Matt asked Ahnalka to perform, but he refused at first.

"He does that to be polite," Matt whispered to me. When Ahnalka was finally persuaded, he asked Ikwah to play the ayayut, a drum made of caribou skin stretched over a bone frame. Ikwah played it by striking the rim with a stick. As Ahnalka sang he swayed from the waist, and at the end he yelled loudly, making Matt and Ikwah laugh.

He then asked Matt to play his concertina and after at first refusing, Matt sang hymns in his strong baritone voice. I always liked to hear him sing—he had livened many an evening on the ship. With smiling, bronze faces and laughter around me, I was happy.

Ahnalka's wife handed me an ivory carving of a walrus. It was so life-like I wished I could have it to take home to Aunt Bessie. I asked Matt, "Can I buy it? I mean trade?"

"It's a gift." He thanked her and I smiled and nodded at her. What a treasure! I resolved to bring her a needle (a treasure to her) and some of Charley's bread.

When the "feast" was over, Matt offered to show me inside an abandoned house made of flat rocks and turf. We took a lamp and crouched to squeeze through a 15-foot tunnel, then climbed up to the floor of a room about ten by twelve feet, and six feet high. Matt pointed to a stone platform built across the back of the room. "The men sit on the edge, the women and children behind them," he said. "And they sleep there, on their furs."

Above the entrance a window let in cloudy light.

I asked what it was made of. "Dried seal intestine," he said. "The small hole in it is a peephole, and it lets heat escape."

I was glad to see how Ahnalka lived in the winter. I thanked Matt for sharing the evening with me, and the next day I wrote a long letter to Aunt Bessie to tell her all I was learning about the Eskimos, and the clever ways they used what was available in their surroundings. I told her, too, how often I thought of her and my comfortable room at home. The letter could be sent back from Etah some time that summer on a whaler. I would take her the ivory walrus later.

In many ways I would soon be living like my hosts, and I was looking forward to having fur clothes like theirs. Matt suggested I ask Kayqueehut if she would make mine. She agreed—all the women were eager to earn some of the expedition's precious prizes of useful tools, and she seemed to like me. She measured me with her hands to make my clothes the right size. On the way to Cape Sheridan she would sew them, and I expected to have them before winter.

The next day I began to wonder if my clothes would last until I got my new furs. When Charley yelled, "It's time to feed the dogs," I went below to get some whale meat, and to my disgust dropped a slab on my pants. I tried to wipe the wet spots off and got my hands smelly, too. "Stinking stuff," I grumbled.

When I got back to the galley, Charley grabbed his nose and yelled, "Take a bath or go jump in the ocean." That made me mad. I washed, but couldn't get the smell out of my pants. At least there was no fog to keep them from drying.

Mr. Peary established a depot of boats, coal and provisions across the bay at Cape Sabine, in case the ship was lost and the explorers had to return by land.

"Would that be possible?" I asked Charley.

"Oh, yes, and we could eventually get home on a whaler. But I hope I never have to walk 350 miles back there from Grant Land, where we're going, and then cross the ice to get back to Greenland. It's a good game region, though—the Commander brought back three musk oxen—eight hundred pounds of fresh beef. At least we wouldn't starve if we had to go that route."

It hadn't occurred to me that I might have to *walk* part of the way home!

CHAPTER 10

One morning I noticed some small floes floating around the ship, and thought it would be fun to ride on them. I grabbed a boat hook and jumped onto one when it hit the ship's side. I vaulted to another ice pan, but jumped too close to the edge, and the whole floe tipped. Quickly I moved to the center to level it. When George saw the fun I was having, he grabbed another boat hook and jumped on a floe nearby. Then he hopped to mine, landing heavily behind me. I yelled, "Blast it! Get off!" I thought we were both going into the water, but we managed to steady our raft.

He vaulted to another, but soon realized he was moving away from the ship and neighboring floes. His comments were more colorful than mine, as he tried hopelessly to use the boat hook as a paddle.

Charley roared at me, "Get back here, you numbskull!" I tried to obey, but the next floe I landed on was thin. To my horror it cracked as I landed, and my feet and legs went through. The icy water hit my stomach and legs. By spreading my arms I stopped myself from going all the way, and prayed the edges of the ice would hold. Charley lowered a boat and came to my rescue. He threw me a rope and hauled me in, but by then my legs were numb. Of course we had an audience on the ship, and George had to wait ten minutes to be picked up. To his embarrassment, the Eskimos laughed and jeered.

After I had had a hot bath, Charley said in a quieter, serious voice, "You won't always be near the ship. Don't try that in winter—it wouldn't take long for you to kill yourself that way if the water gets inside your furs. Even if you hauled yourself out, it would just take longer to die from the cold." He made me feel like a naughty child.

To save weight the expedition carried no canned meat except pemmican for the trek to the Pole. The Commander relied on hunting to supply us. He sent parties out to get more walrus meat for the Eskimos and the dogs, and they were successful. One of the crew brought home a live baby walrus. He left it tied on the shore while the meat was unloaded, and

Ooqueah and I went to see it. The little fellow was about four feet long. As we approached, it turned its ugly head toward us, making guttural sounds and pulling against its anchor. When we came closer, it yanked the line so hard it came loose, and the little beast headed for the water.

"Arretit! Stop!" Ooqueah yelled, and started after him. He picked up the end of the line dragging behind it and leaned backward, but the walrus was too strong. Ooqueah fell to the ground and was pulled along. "Help!" he cried. When he dug in his heels, they made furrows in the gravel.

I was right behind him and ran to grab the rope just ahead of his hands. I had to dig in my heels, too, and together we managed to stop the beast before it got to the water. "Some baby! He's as strong as an ox," I said, brushing the gravel off my pants. We had to leave the animal there—we couldn't drag it back—but Ooqueah anchored it more firmly.

I was dying to go hunting and especially wanted to see how the Eskimos speared walrus. Charley said I could go if I could find room in a boat. We chose to go with Ikwah and Ooqueah and six other Eskimos. In the morning George got us a whaleboat and sat in the stern to guide the rowers. As I climbed in, I looked forward to an adventure, a welcome relief from my chores.

The Eskimos quickly learned to handle the unfamiliar boat. Ikwah pointed far out to where a herd of walruses was sunning on an ice floe. We hoped to get close quietly before they saw us. But George was taking pictures and forgot to give the order to stop rowing, so the animals woke and began to slide into the water. Ikwah stood in the bow, harpoon in his right hand. A sealskin line was attached to the pointed harpoon tip. Ooqueah fastened the loose end to the bow of the whaleboat. George and I started firing, but the bullets seemed to have no effect.

"Tough skins," George yelled.

"Shoot just behind eyes," Ooqueah advised. "Ahwick has a thick hide, hard skull. But we must get close to stab it, or they sink."

Suddenly a huge walrus surfaced close to the boat. I gasped at the size of it. Ikwah lunged and with all his strength thrust his harpoon into it, then withdrew the shaft, leaving the tip buried in the neck of the walrus. The frightened beast bellowed and turned away.

As it thrashed through the water, the walrus began to tow us. We scraped a floe, and the boat tipped. George yelled as though he were cheering a race horse. He fired once, but missed. I hung on, afraid we would smash into the ice or overturn—I certainly didn't want to be in the water with that wounded monster. Ooqueah moved forward with a knife, ready to cut the bow line if the walrus went under the ice.

As soon as Ikwah finished tying an inflated sealskin to the harpoon line as a float, Ooqueah let the walrus go. When it grew tired we could find it. After I calmed down and got my breath I said, "That was a wild ride."

"It was a humdinger," George agreed. "Let's go get another beast."

As the boat turned, Ikwah shouted, "Ahwick tedicksoah! Many walrus!"

I saw with horror that our bullets had wounded and angered the herd, and they were charging toward the whaleboat, churning the water and croaking, "Ook! Ook!" With hoarse bellows they lifted half of their huge bodies out of the water and crashed again, making waves that threatened to tip us over. They sounded like a cage-full of roaring lions. I was so scared I could hardly hold my gun steady—I thought we were doomed. Ikwah rattled his harpoon handle against the bow and screamed to frighten them, while the rowers beat the animals' heads with the oars to keep them from ramming the boat. They were all around us.

We kept firing and managed to hit the fatal spot a couple of times, but one walrus hit the hull right beside me, knocking me off balance. I looked into the bloodshot eyes of the beast two feet away from me. Long hairs bristled on its thick lips. Its breath smelled sour. I backed away. The monster roared and raised its gleaming white tusks above the gunwale. Just as they were about to hook over the side of the boat, George fired. The creature spat a mouthful of water and clam shells in my face. Jupiter! That was too close. Ikwah harpooned it before it sank.

We kept firing until the herd finally retreated. I was almost out of ammunition. After I stopped shaking, I asked Ooqueah, "How do you do this in a kayak and without guns? I was scared witless—that last one would have tipped us over."

Ooqueah said, "We catch them sleeping on the ice, but it can happen." I didn't like to think about that. George and I started to bail. Thank goodness for the double hull, or the walrus would have made a hole clear through. We hauled the dead walrus to a floe and went after the one marked with the float. After we pulled it onto the ice I watched Ikwah skin it with a small knife, cutting the meat off without striking bone. The Eskimos packed it into the whaleboat.

As harpooner, Ikwah would get the largest share—he chose the head, the left flipper and the heart. We left the second one for a later trip. That day my respect for the fearless Inuit hunters grew, and I realized how important the reward of a gun was to them.

When we returned, I told Matt, "That was the fright of my life. I didn't think we'd get home alive."

"You should never have gone out without other boats nearby," he said in an angry voice. "There's nothing more dangerous than a herd of walruses."

"Never again," I promised. I was sorry to have upset him, but sometimes I got tired of being the only "child" on board. I didn't want to make mistakes. And I'm sure he didn't scold George.

In the next two days Matt and some Eskimos shot and recovered four walruses, and the crew of the *Erik* supplied forty-two more to feed the expedition and the Eskimos. They carved them up, using the deck as a slaughterhouse. It was a horrible, bloody scene, and I had to help swab the deck down afterward. That night we had baked stuffed walrus heart—Charley's specialty. It was chewy but good.

Mr. Mac and I took two boatloads of bones to the dogs, where they had been put ashore on an island to run free until departure time. We had to unload in a hurry or we would have been buried under a pack of hungry, snapping dogs. On the way back to the ship it started snowing and continued the next day, when everyone started preparing for the journey to Cape Sheridan.

CHAPTER 11

Matt called to me. "Want to help me fix the Crow's Nest?" He knew I liked to climb the rigging. I scrambled up the main mast, and we reinforced the barrel at the top. I lined it with fur so it would protect the Captain when he stayed aloft to search for the best route to attack the ice—he would be bounced around up there. Then Matt put me to work re-stowing the cargo on deck securely. "Have to be in fighting trim to get through the ice," he said.

After the crew filled the boilers with fresh water and cleaned the furnaces, the Inuit transferred 550 tons of coal and 70 tons of whale and walrus meat from the *Erik* to the *Roosevelt*. The Commander left fifty tons of coal at Etah for our return trip. The Doctor and Mr. Mac stocked the whaleboats with food and medical supplies in case we lost the ship—in each boat they put a tent, stove and oil, guns, sails and all kinds of tools. We all wrote letters for the *Erik* to take home.

The Commander warned us, "From now on there will be serious work; up to now it's been easy." That surprised me—I thought I had been working hard. Then I realized he meant the battle with ice ahead of us. The tales I had heard of crushed ships had aggravated my dreams, and now danger was close at hand—we must steam 350 miles up Kennedy and Robeson Channels to the Polar Sea. How difficult would our passage be?

Before we could leave there was one more chore—the mikkies (dogs) must be brought to the ship from their island. Matt directed the excursion, and we all helped, but getting them into the whaleboat was not easy. George and I grabbed each dog by the neck and struggled to force it aboard, while it squirmed and bit. When our boat was full of snarling, fighting animals, we rowed back to the ship. The Eskimos wrapped a rope around each yelping dog and hauled it up and over the rail on the port side. The pigs and sheep vanished in panic toward the stern. We tied 246 dogs down on deck, but not so tightly that they couldn't fight, which they did constantly.

"Why do we need so many?" I asked Matt.

"We lose sixty percent of them," he explained—

"some from exhaustion or illness. And the Eskimos taught us that when meat is used up on the trail, we can feed dogs to dogs, and if necessary to us. The Commander and I wouldn't be here today if we hadn't sacrificed one on the trip over the Greenland ice cap. The meat and the seal's blood Analka gave me to drink when we returned saved my life." I stared at him. There were horror stories he hadn't told me.

As I watched the dogs, I hated the idea that some had to die. What a sacrifice of these strong animals! The thought of losing so many shocked me. I knew Ooqueah loved his dogs. Would they survive? I cared about all of them, especially Karko. She was the same color as Molly and was friendly— she let me scratch her ears. It would be terrible to lose her. Could Ooqueah kill her to save his life?

In addition to our regular crew, twenty-two Eskimo men, seventeen women, and ten children came aboard, as well as dogs, hunting equipment, twenty sixteen-foot kayaks, tents, pots, lamps, and grass for bedding. I wondered how I could move around. When things settled down, I thought of those left behind. What a big change that would make for them, too! The tribe of 220 would be reduced to 171 when the Commander took some of them away with us for a whole year.

On August 18 I woke to miserable weather—snow and rain, with a strong gale blowing across Smith Sound. As the ship began the last stage of its journey, we headed for Ellesmere Island on the other side of the channel. Now our company was complete, and there was nothing ahead but a new kind of wilderness. We would be isolated.

I found comfort on deck was impossible. It was frustrating to step carefully through the clutter, and the coal scattered fine dust everywhere. With such a full load aboard, the noise and filth were hard to bear, and each day it got worse. I heard others grumbling, and swearing at the Eskimos, who had no regular times to sleep or eat. The staff often escaped to the mess room for privacy.

To provide some relief, the Captain announced, "When you hear the ship's bell at 10 p.m., you must be quiet. Another at 12 p.m. means all lights go out." Matt explained to the Eskimos to be sure they understood. I was thankful for the rule—it was hard enough anyway to go to sleep in twilight.

After living with the dogs for several days I didn't think of them as noble any more. Spirited? Yes—they loved to fight. They snarled and bit and growled , but they didn't bark—they howled at all hours. And they made such an awful stinking mess. Matt saw me frowning at the dirty deck and said,

"Get used to it, Tom. There's no way around the problem." I chose to climb through the rigging to move fore or aft, even though I had to avoid the walrus meat hanging there.

Kayqueehut was working on my furs. She had prepared skins by scraping fat off the hides and drying them in the sun and wind. I had seen her chewing the fat out of them—if any oil was left in the suit it would freeze. She folded a piece of deer-skin, popped it in her mouth and chewed on it, refolding it frequently, until it was soft. After a day of chewing, she would take a day off to rest her jaws. This seemed to be a constant chore for all women, and I noticed that as a result their teeth were shorter than the men's.

As if that weren't strange enough, I saw that when Kayqueehut started to sew, she squatted on the deck, raised one bare foot and held the end of a piece of fur between her big and second toes, using them like fingers on a third hand. She looked so strange in that position with her foot in the air in front of her that I couldn't help laughing. I don't know how she kept her balance for such a long time—she seemed to be sitting on one hip. I went to get George to share my amusement.

"What practical ways Eskimos use to get jobs done!" he said.

The comical sight brought to mind a contrasting one of Aunt Bessie sitting primly in her chair, daintily sewing tiny stitches in a delicate fabric. I wanted to remember to tell her about my seamstress, so I drew a picture of Kayqueehut with her three "hands."

For several days we made good progress through Kennedy Channel. When spray broke high over the bow, I heard Ikwah mutter, "The devil is spitting." On the fifth day we made 100 miles, but soon the Captain had to guide the ship close to shore to avoid moving ice in the channel, and often the ship scraped bottom.

To keep their attention away from their fears, the Commander had each Eskimo man build his own sledge and make harnesses. Matt had to supervise the making of two dozen new sledges and have them ready for use at Cape Sheridan. I watched him file and polish "shoes" for the oak runners—two-inch-wide steel strips.

"You can help," he said. He showed me how to bind two-foot-long boards six inches apart between the runners to form a strong base, using rawhide lashings. "Nails aren't flexible, and they would rust," he explained.

The Peary sledges were thirteen and a half feet long—bigger and stronger than the ones Eskimos had made out of walrus shoulder blades and whale ribs until the Commander brought them wood.

"How heavy a load do you carry?" I asked.

"These will carry 1000 pounds, but we'll each take 500 to the Pole."

I remembered what Captain Bartlett had told me. On the ice cap trip in Greenland, Matt drove sixteen dogs, pulling a load of a thousand pounds on a three-runner sledge. Peary, in the lead, slowed him down, so he pulled Peary's sledge behind him as a trailer and drove a twenty-eight-dog team. It sounded impossible, but Matt was expert at many things.

He interrupted my thoughts. "If you learn to handle the dogs, I'm sure the Commander can use your help moving supplies," he said. That promise made me so excited I stayed awake that night. I resolved to do everything I could to make myself stronger.

CHAPTER 12

Sixty-nine people had lived in close quarters on board for so long! When I was irritated I had tried to follow the example of the staff members and not complain, but I lost my temper sometimes, mostly about the mess on deck. The crew bickered now and then, but a real fight broke out only once. An Eskimo we called "Harrigan," who especially liked to tease, got on the nerves of one of the crewmen. I heard a commotion and loud language; Harrigan left the fo'c'sle moaning, with a hand over his eye.

"Not a fair fight," Matt commented. "The Eskimos don't know anything about boxing."

Harrigan went to Mr. Peary. The Commander always soothed the Eskimos and tried to keep them happy, for fear of losing his helpers. He gave Harrigan a small knife, which seemed to satisfy him.

Soon there were more important things to worry

about. As we entered Robeson Channel I realized the Captain had a new problem. When the tide flowed north, the ship could go forward a few miles, but when it ebbed and rushed toward us, the Captain sometimes had to hide her in a niche at the shore to avoid being driven backward by ice. The Commander knew every mile of the shoreline and could tell him where to go. But in one ebb tide as we entered a cove, an iceberg rammed us against the shore.

I grabbed the rail as the ship listed to starboard and everything not tied down began to slide. When the ice froze around us, Mr. Peary ordered the crew to loosen it with dynamite. I held my breath as the crew brought the dynamite up from the hold. The Commander showed the crew where to bury it. I remarked to George, "Isn't that awfully close?"

"Relax. I'm sure he's done this before," he answered.

The crew wrapped several pieces of dynamite and fastened them to the end of a pole. They connected a wire to them and thrust the pole down through cracks in the ice at several places nearby. When they connected the other ends of the wires to a battery, I stepped back and covered my ears, but George gleefully yelled "POW!" at each explosion. The ship shuddered at the blasts, as water and pieces of ice shot a hundred feet into the air.

When the tide rose, it loosened a great pile of ice, and the Captain was able to move the ship. A short time later we looked back to the spot where the ship had been caught. Blocks of ice were piled up thirty feet high. Not even this vessel could have survived there.

The safest place to tie up was behind a piece of a glacier where it was stranded ashore. Often the ship was held fast until the pack outside shifted. While we were waiting for the tide to turn one day, Ooqueah invited me to go fishing at a lake.

I asked Charley if I could go. He said, "Fresh fish would be welcome. But if you hear the steam whistle, scramble back here fast."

The lake was less than a mile inland—children had been hauling water from it to the ship. The land was flat for a long way and the snow was not deep. Ooqueah didn't like snowshoes, so we walked. He carried only his pickax, a spear with sharp pieces of deer antler set in the end, and a fishing line made of braided sealskin sinew.

"Where's the bait?" I asked.

He showed me a small piece of ivory carved like a fish, attached it to the line, cut a hole in the ice and dropped it in. We didn't wait long before a fish came up to look. He speared it—a huge char—

and threw it on the ice, where it flopped until he stunned it.

"You try," he said, handing me the spear. When another fish appeared, I tried but missed. "You waited too long," he said.

The second time I was lucky, and landed the biggest fish I had ever caught—about twelve pounds. That was the best day I had had in a while.

When we were through, Ooqueah cut out pieces of fish to eat raw. I tasted some—it was sweeter than I expected. It tasted even better when Charley cooked the fish that night. They were a special treat for everyone. But I hated being back on the ship. Getting away from the stench and noise had been a wonderful relief, and I thanked Ooqueah for the adventure. It was fun to be with him.

At Shelter River, Professor Marvin called me to the rail and pointed. "That's the place where the *Roosevelt* got caught between the pack ice and the ice-foot on our last journey. Her stern post was smashed and the rudder cracked. The ice sheared off two blades of the propeller. We thought she wouldn't survive." The Professor's tale reminded me that things could get worse.

The next time we were tied up on shore, I was

working in the galley when I realized the ship was turning and moving southward. I ran forward to see what was happening. The tide had sent our huge berg adrift and it was pulling us.

"Unhook the cable!" the Captain shouted. One end of it was securely buried on the berg; the other was fastened on board rather than to the hull to save time in just such an emergency. The crew loosened it and let it go before we had drifted far.

One of them remarked, "On the last trip we lost an anchor—it's easier to replace the cable."

The Chief had started the engines, but we were still in the pack ice we had tried to escape. As a big berg passed on our port side, I stared in fear at an even bigger one coming at us to starboard. Surely we would be caught between them. The Captain could find no way out—I cowered in the galley as the ice closed in, and cringed when it ground against the hull. The ship creaked with the pressure. I was horrified to see a spur of the berg smash the after rail into splinters. Every plank was complaining, and sharp reports of pressured boards sounded like bones cracking. I shuddered and stared in horror as the rigging became slack and the deck actually bulged upward. Some of the crew placed emergency supplies at the rail to be thrown over if necessary. Were we really going to lose our home?

Charlie yelled, "Grab your emergency kit!" Everyone had a bundle handy in case we had to abandon ship. I got mine from the cabin and was ready to leap, but how could we be safe in a whaleboat in the moving ice? When I had watched the boats loaded with supplies, I hadn't really believed they would be needed.

Just when it seemed the hull would crack, the ship's slanting sides helped her to rise, and she popped up like a slippery eel, rescuing herself. I started breathing again. After a few minutes the starboard iceberg moved on, and we slid into open water. Captain Bartlett headed for another safer place to tie up. Still shaking, I went back to the galley.

The following day, solid ice stood in our way, so the Captain climbed to the Crow's Nest 100 feet above the water to take charge. When he ordered "Full steam ahead," I clung to the rigging to watch—now we would see what the *Roosevelt* could do. The ship gathered speed, rushed forward and crashed against the ice. The narrow steel-shod bow split it and sent pieces flying to the sides. Black smoke poured from the stack. The crew cheered, the dogs howled, and the Eskimos shrieked in fear.

The Captain bellowed from his high perch through a four-foot megaphone lashed to the side of the barrel and aimed at the wheel. His orders were relayed to the engine room. "Smash 'em! Split 'em in two! Go to it!" he yelled. His loud voice seemed to come from a deep well in his chest. He jumped up and down and swore as the mast swayed. Ootah, looking up at the Captain, said, "He piblocto!" He did look kind of crazy.

When the ice didn't crack, the slanted bow let the ship rise over it and come to rest on the ice pan, with her nose pointed skyward. Was she stuck there? No,

she started to slide back, and the Captain shouted, "Full speed astern! Now, again! Full speed ahead!" The dogs got excited, too, interrupting him by howling. He had to shout his order again. As we made repeated attacks, I grew more excited. What a ship! Now I understood why the Commander designed a special one for this journey.

With each thump of ice the Eskimos chanted, calling on the souls of their ancestors for help. When we felt a tremendous jolt underneath the hull they screamed, believing the blows were warnings from Tornarsuk. Matt reassured them. "Those thumps are huge pieces of ice that have been pushed down. When we break up the surface, they pop up from underneath."

Progress was slow. "Used up two tons of coal going the last fifty feet," the Mate growled. At that rate, I wondered if we'd have enough coal to get home. This went on for days. I don't know how the Captain or the Commander got any sleep. I got very little—it was impossible for any of us when the ship was in action. The days were getting shorter, but seemed long because we slept so little.

As we approached the end of Robeson Channel on September 5th, the sloping headland of Cape Sheridan on the northern coast of Ellesmere Island came into view.

CHAPTER 13

The 251 miles from Etah to the Cape had taken 19 days. I was relieved that the ship's battle with the ice was over—we had arrived safely and on time, farther north than any ship had gone before. Now I could see the bluish ice pans of the Polar Sea stretching to the horizon. It was a bleak sight, but to the south of me were some bare patches of reddish-brown land between areas of dazzling white snow. In the mountains, shadows of many colors filled the ravines, and pink clouds drifted on the wind.

I could feel the excitement among the crew. The Commander put Eskimo families to work hauling supplies up from the holds to be ready for landing. After two weeks of fighting ice, he and the Captain looked exhausted. Charley and I watched as the Captain inched the *Roosevelt* ashore and the mooring lines went out onto the stable ice sheet attached fast to land. Excitement mounted as we began to unload. We put the dogs ashore first, and they ran and leaped happily on the shelf ice. The sailors washed down the deck; then all hands unloaded the twenty-four new sledges, food and equipment.

We hauled everything to the shore, so if the ship was damaged or went adrift, we still had supplies and could return by land. The crew stacked the hunks of whale meat in great piles in the snow, and George and I barricaded them with dozens of bags of coal. I had to get used to a steady surface under my feet again, but what a relief to have space to walk and run!

While I was carrying coal ashore, I heard cries of alarm and saw men running toward Marvin, who stood facing a hole in the ice. I dropped the coal and followed them. George was there ahead of me. "Holy Moses!" he shouted. "His sledge broke through. There goes our ammunition. The whole load sank."

I stared at the hole, then at the shock on all the faces around me. If we couldn't hunt we'd starve. While crewmen brought ropes to recover the load, Matt warned us to stand back in case more of the ice broke. "I don't know why all of it was loaded on one sledge," he said.

The water was not deep, and the crew soon had the cases out. We waited in suspense until they opened one. When we heard a glad shout, "It's dry!" we all cheered. How fortunate that those cases were really waterproof! The crew stored the explosives safely away from the settlement and over-turned the whaleboats for the winter. Five days later, when everything was ashore, I wondered how the ship had carried it all.

At a high tide the Captain was able to move the floating empty ship closer to shore, safely placing her behind stranded icebergs to avoid any pressure from the pack ice. This would be my home for the winter. And now it was clean! From the galley I could see the way to the North Pole—a jumble of ice. When the sun returned in the spring it would take two months at least for the Commander to travel there and back.

We set up the larger tents and Professor Marvin showed us how to build temporary houses. That was fun. He told us, "To make the walls, stack the boxes of provisions on their sides, so the tops open into the room; then we can get at the contents easily. We'll use spars and sails to make the roof."

"This house is like a grocery store!" George exclaimed in wonder. I took note of where the co-coa was stored.

The crew set all the sails to dry in the wind before storing them for the winter. The *Roosevelt,* held fast in the ice but under full sail, was a magnificent sight. I got George to take a picture of it. Everyone was excited and full of energy, and Mr. Peary was humming a tune. George dumped snow down my neck. "I'll get you!" I shouted as I tried to wash his face with snow. I couldn't make snowballs—the snow was either as dry as granulated sugar, or packed solid by the wind.

"Let's try out the snowshoes and I'll race you back to the ship," he said. The Arctic snowshoes were different from mine at home—six feet long and one foot wide, built for crossing new thin ice. George gave me a head start, but I stumbled and fell on my face. He looked back and stood there, laughing. "Lift your toes, Big Foot!" he yelled. He got to the ship ten yards ahead of me. "I'll race you again when you've grown up," he teased. I took a mock swing at his chin; then we went to the galley to get a hot drink.

Mr. Peary made it clear that hunting was most important. He sent parties out in different directions to get fresh meat, and they returned with the skins and meat of musk oxen, hares and caribou.

The Eskimos saved the antlers—they had many uses for bone. The women set their fox traps along the shore for miles.

One day I got my chance to go hunting with Matt and Dr. Goodsell. We took two Eskimos and sledges with us and headed south toward the mountains. By noontime I heard a shout, "Oomingmuksue!" and saw black dots in the distance—a small herd of musk oxen about a mile away.

The dogs yelped and strained at their harnesses. When Matt freed two, they raced toward the herd. The musk oxen backed up in a half circle against a cliff, tails together. As we got closer I could see their thick coats of long, coarse hairs, dark brown except for cream-colored spots high on their shoulders and backs. The ends blew in the wind like a

heavy skirt. The Inuit name for it was accurate—
"animal with skin like a beard." The fur of their
legs, barely showing beneath, was almost white.
As the dogs rushed toward them, they lowered their
sharp horns.

"Aim at the base of the skull or behind the front
shoulder," Matt said. "It's no good to aim at the
head because of the huge knobby base of the horns."

A bull charged the dogs; I fired, but missed. Matt
shot, and the bull fell. Another musk ox charged,
and the Doctor brought it down. Finally I hit one in
the right spot and felt pretty proud of myself.

We had to tie the excited dogs down while the
Eskimos cut up the animals. Skinning them was a
hard job. The hair was thickly matted—it stuck to
the blood freezing on the knives and made cutting
difficult. Under the outer hairs there was a layer of
yellowish wool which the Eskimos called "qiviut."
They carefully saved it. When the men had cut the
meat from the bones and packed it on the sledges,
the dogs fought over what was thrown to them. I
was glad we had some food for them to replace
some whale meat that had spoiled.

When we ate our lunch, Matt handed me something he called a vacuum bottle. It was cold on the
outside, but he poured steaming tea out of it—so
hot it burned my mouth, and I cooled it a little

with ice. Imagine having a hot drink without carrying a stove! What an invention! That was something almost as novel as shooting a musk ox.

My next hunt, late in the month, was with Ooqueah, who needed more sealskin. He could no longer hunt from a kayak. We took his sledge and team out on the ice to look for a hole where a seal would come to take a fresh breath. It wasn't long before his dogs were in a circle, all their noses pointed at the same spot. They had found a breathing hole. I was surprised to see how small it was—just big enough for a seal's head. Ooqueah tied the dogs at a distance, and we sat on cakes of ice with our feet on a piece of fur.

"Don't move. Seals have good ears," he explained.

We waited and waited. It seemed like hours before one came to the hole; it took a quick breath and left. "It will be back if it doesn't hear any noises," Ooqueah whispered. And sure enough the seal came again, and the third time stayed longer to breathe. Ooqueah quickly speared it in the head. While the seal thrashed around under the ice, I chopped the hole in the ice bigger so we could pull it out.

Ooqueah cut the skin vertically in a single line from mouth to tail flipper, then peeled off the blubber in one piece. After making another deeper slit, he saved the liver, intestines and other organs and fed the rest of the innards to the dogs. To him, the choice parts were the liver and the eyes, which he ate raw. I tried the liver, but when he offered me an eye, I let him eat both of them. I helped him store everything on the sledge—he would make use of the skin, bones, blubber and meat.

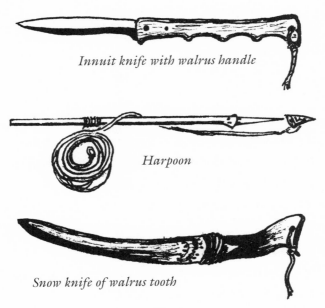

Innuit knife with walrus handle

Harpoon

Snow knife of walrus tooth

CHAPTER 14

All the tenderfoot members were as eager as I was to learn to harness the dogs and drive a team. Matt said that all supplies must be carried 93 miles to the west, to Cape Columbia. "Why are they to be taken there?" I asked.

"That land base is closest to the Pole. The Commander chose it because on our last trip, while we were waiting for days at the Big Lead, the sea ice drifted east. When we were able to cross, we came ashore in Greenland."

It seemed the Commander, too, had learned many things the hard way, just as we all did. At least his experience helped us avoid some problems. I began to realize that I had a lot more to learn if I wanted to take part in moving some equipment. Fortunately there was plenty of time before spring.

When there was enough snow, Matt and the Eskimos started hauling. The assistants began to collect the dogs and form teams to practice with. Ooqueah came to me with his sledge and offered to show me how to drive the dogs. That was a break—I couldn't ask for a better teacher.

"First get the harness on," he said. He threw a piece of meat to a male dog. I made a dive for the hundred-pound animal, and straddled him. Grabbing him with one bare hand I tried to slip the sealskin harness over his head. The dog bit me and ran off with the piece of meat. I tried again; this time I threw my entire weight across his back, and put an arm under him. The dog struggled, but I finally pulled the straps over his head and pushed his forepaws through the opening for the chest.

Ooqueah fastened the dog's trace, a fifteen-foot rawhide line, to his leather harness and wrapped the other end around a rock, while I worked with another dog. For a loaded sledge I would need seven or eight. It took hours to harness six, and by then I was exhausted. They had to be left alone while they decided who was fit to be king of the team. I rested while the males fought and the three females watched. I remembered what Matt had said—"The winner is king. He rules with a look or a growl."

The frame of Ooqueah's sledge, his old kamutee, was built from pieces of driftwood lashed together. I had seen him use a wooden drill, fitted with a bone bit. Until the Commander gave the tribe a few modern tools, I imagine cutting all the holes for the lacings had taken him hours.

I fastened the dogs' 15-foot traces to a toggle, a small ring in the middle of a bridle line stretched between the runners of the sledge. I could see this gave the dogs more freedom to spread out. If one slipped or fell into a hole in the sea ice, the others wouldn't overrun him or be in the same danger.

I thought the hard part of this lesson was done, but no, learning to use the whip and make the dogs obey was a lot more difficult than driving a team of horses. Ooqueah tried to show me how to use my arm and wrist to snap the twenty-five foot walrus-hide whip. The lash wasn't meant to hurt—a snap over the ears of a dog and the threat of pain was supposed to make him move.

I shouted "Huk! Huk!" and tried to crack the whip, but the length of it made it awkward to handle. It snapped back and hit my sleeve. The lead dog didn't move—he yawned. This was going to take longer than I expected. I aimed the whip lower, but it just raised a cloud of snow. Ooqueah shouted at the dogs and motioned for me to throw my weight against the upstanders. I pushed the sledge, and when the huskies started off, I ran beside it—there was no platform at the back to stand on. I was supposed to control the dogs with my whip and voice: How-eh (to the left), ash-ook (to the right), ka-ka (keep going) or eye-eye (stop).

"Shout louder. Get their attention," Ooqueah instructed. I bellowed, "Howeh! Howeh!" and snapped the whip again. It lashed back and tripped me, and I fell on my face. Ooqueah yelled to the dogs; he laughed so hard he sat down and rolled in the snow. I was embarrassed, but he made me laugh, too. I quit for that day, promising Ooqueah I would try again. He had been so patient.

The next day I watched Eskimo boys practicing with their whips. They lined up the frozen bodies of dogs that had died. Gruesome, but I was learning that they didn't waste anything. Some of the youngsters could hit close to any head in the group. I showed George. "That's the best way to learn— less embarrassing and easier on me and the dogs."

"Yeah. Good idea," he agreed.

When I had practiced and improved, I tried driving the team again with a Peary sledge. The huskies started off, and I was feeling more confident. But soon two dogs headed for snow easier to run through, and as they jumped over nearby dogs, they tangled the lines. I stopped and undid their traces. While I was unsnarling them, they got away from me and headed for the ship. I had to go after them and face the laughter and teasing of the Eskimos. Would I ever learn?

Professor Marvin tried to make me feel better. "The Eskimos judge us by how well we do the things they're good at. They like to feel superior. And we know all too well that they are better than we are at Arctic skills—we dread their scorn. But don't forget you can teach them things, too."

"What?" I asked. What did I have to offer? "Only how to use a toothbrush," I said in sarcasm. I recovered the dogs, hitched them again to the loaded sledge and kept working with them until I made fewer mistakes.

Several days later I was dismayed to learn that one of Ooqueah's dogs had died. They were as unpredictable as the weather. They were quite comfortable sleeping in the snow and chewing it for their water, and they would rather run than sleep. They worked well in severe weather, even though on the trail the Eskimos fed them only once in three days. It was strange that in good weather and after a good meal, they would suddenly lie down and die.

It was a special day when Kayqueehut brought me my new furs. I thanked her, and rewarded her with soap, a loaf of Charley's good bread and a needle. After that she smiled at me every time I

Mary Irwin

saw her. Matt gave me some good advice: "Hang
the furs out in the sun and wind for a while to get
rid of the lice. They'll freeze and you can beat them
out. You'll get dirty enough without having to put
up with the beasties."

When I had done that, I took off my light sheepskin jacket and tried on the deerskin kooletah. The
sleeves were large and the back was loose so I could
pull my arms and hands inside to get them warm.
A drawstring, run through a loop at the back of
the jacket, pulled the front and back flaps snugly
between my legs so no wind or water could get
inside. The hood was made of bearskin, with a ruff
of fox fur to protect my face. I marveled at the
design and at the sewing—the stitches were so close

together they completely covered the seams.

My new pants were of bearskin also. They reached just below my knees. "It's important not to perspire and then get chilled," Matt warned. "The air vents at the knees will keep you from getting too hot. In the coldest weather you can cover them with strips of foxtail."

The long socks were made from the pelts of Arctic hares, with the fur on the inside. They felt wonderfully warm. The high boots (kamiks) were reindeer skin, with the fur removed. I could tie them tight at the top, just under my knees, where they covered my pants. Another lighter pair was made from sealskin. Bearskin mittens and another pair of deerskin, soft as velvet, completed my outfit. Ooqueah gave me two bands of fur to wear on my wrists, over my pulse, to help keep me warm. I knew ice water on the wrists could cool me, but I hadn't tried getting warmer this way.

"Put dried grass in your socks and between them and your boots; it will absorb moisture and keep your feet dry," Matt advised. "If you stay dry you won't get frostbite. Remember that, Tom, because I'm sure you can help us take loads to the Cape. You have learned to handle the dogs well enough."

His promise restored my confidence. This was what I had hoped for. I could escape from the ship occasionally, since Charley didn't have to cook for many people, and a chance to be an assistant on land would be a reward for the hours of practice with the whip.

On September 16th the fall sledging started. The Commander broke us in by sending us on short trips to stations on the way to the Cape. He put each tenderfoot in charge of three Eskimos, to manage them and their teams of dogs. That would be difficult, I thought, since the Inuit were the experts. On the trail we learned how to wear our new clothes, handle the dogs and get used to sledging and weather conditions.

CHAPTER 15

On the first trip George was in charge of Ooqueah, another Eskimo called Panikpah, and me. Ooqueah had let me have my favorite dog Karko as part of my team. I was glad she was female and didn't have to fight. I carefully packed a four-hundred-pound load on my Peary-type sledge, with the weight low. The pemmican tins were the same length as the width of the sledge, and formed the floor. On this I lashed other food and equipment to be moved to the cache.

I was impatient to leave. When George was ready, my dogs were rearing on their hind legs, eager to go, but they could not start the sledge alone—I had to use all my strength to move it. The dogs then leaned into their harnesses, shoulders forward, tails curved over their backs. The load was much heavier than anything I had hauled in practice; keeping it upright on a rough trail was the toughest job I had tackled yet. I fell behind. Some of the dogs seemed to delight in weaving their lines together. I had to untangle traces with my bare hands, while they jumped and barked and snapped at me.

I wasn't the only one having trouble. I saw some of the assistants beat them with whip handles or snowshoes to make them move after a stop. An Eskimo driver was more likely to get on top of the dog and chew his pointed ear.

On the march, the snow began drifting. Though the dogs' wide hairy feet usually kept them from sinking, now the snow was up to their chests. When I stood still for a moment, the wind piled the snow up against my legs. It crept higher and higher. "Gee Whillikers! It's trying to bury me!" I hollered to Ooqueah.

"Keep moving," he answered. I did, but it was a struggle.

The dogs were tired, and progress was slow. Ooqueah yelled, "Arretit! Turn the sledge over." He made a circle with his hand. I did as he asked, and when the runners were uppermost and level, he removed his mitts and took a mouthful of snow. As it melted, he dripped some from his bare hand on the bottom of a runner and spread it with a piece of polar bear fur. In a few moments both runners were iced. While he warmed his hands under his kooletah, I tightened the load. When we started off, the dogs sprang ahead more easily.

"That worked wonders," I said, gratefully.

At the end of the day my long woolen underwear was soaked with perspiration. My new clothes had been hot, and I had been too busy to remember to use the vents to avoid that. George and I were tired, but Panikpah was still full of energy. We put up the tent as quickly as we could, using sledge runners instead of tent pegs to hold the sides down. The tent floor was sewed to the sides. We closed the opening by a drawstring.

As soon as we finished, George said, "Let's eat!" Panikpah just added hot water to his raw venison. He called it "ki-al." I called it weak soup. George and I boiled our meat and then speared pieces with our hunting knives—we had no forks on this trip, and only one spoon for four of us.

While we were eating, the dogs set up a clamor. We dashed out to find that one had chewed his trace to escape and was breaking into a tin of pemmican. I recalled that Mr. Peary had warned, "Always keep the teams harnessed and tied down. If there's any food around, they'll find it—they even chew leather and tin."

Now I believed it. We retied the dog and I tasted

the pemmican before feeding the rest of it to the other dogs. It was a mixture of chopped-up dried beef, fat, sugar, and raisins or other fruit. It wasn't bad. "What will meals be like out on the polar ice?" I asked George.

He looked skeptical. "They will all be the same, and we won't be doing any cooking—we'll have to eat the pemmican frozen or dunk it in hot tea. We won't go hungry though, and the Commander says it's a healthful meal—it will keep us from getting scurvy."

It didn't sound appetizing to me.

During that night, my first in a tent in the Arctic, I couldn't sleep. The noises of the ice were closer than when we were on the ship, and the dogs howled and fought right outside. It was so cold the oil stove burned all night.

In the morning the Eskimos stepped outside and stood still, or moved very slowly and stiff-legged when loading their sledges.

"What's the matter?" I asked.

Ooqueah explained that he was waiting for his kamiks to freeze in the right shape. I understood too well when mine didn't—they had been soft and moist from condensation; now they froze bent at the toes. Ooqueah laughed to see me walking like a clown. "When are you going to grow up and walk like an Inuit?" he teased.

That made me angry and I yelled at him, "Blast it! Nobody told me about this!" I went back to relight the oil stove to thaw them.

Before long I had some really bad luck. The sun was lower now and later in rising. When we were driving in twilight, it was hard to see the ridges ahead. Suddenly, as the dogs swerved, the front of the sledge hit a mound of ice and stopped. To my horror the bridle line snapped and the dogs kept running, dragging their traces.

"Follow them!" I yelled to Panikpah. Desperately I tried to move the sledge, but left it and ran after the Eskimo at top speed. I must have run a mile before I saw the dogs ahead of me. Some of them had tried to go around a pillar of ice to the left, some to the right, so their traces, still fastened to the toggle, had caught and stopped them. Panikpah had anchored his team behind a ridge and was trying to untangle mine.

George came back toward us and started to scold Panikpah in his usual vivid language. The young man understood his tone if not the words. I stepped between them and said, "Panikpah was just trying to help. I was driving." George shrugged his shoulders and calmed down. I suppose he was frustrated because of the delay. I drove the dogs back to the sledge. Panikpah came with me and helped replace the bridle line.

Our partners waited for us out on the ice shelf, where they were facing some cracks. As we came near, George decided to cross a narrow one. The dogs leapt over it, but the far edge of the ice snapped off, and they slid back into the water, splashing with their forepaws. George lunged toward the sledge and halted the heavy load just before it went in after them. While we watched breathlessly, he found firm footing, and one by one dragged the dogs out by their traces. We gave a cheer. Anyone else would probably have lost the team and the sledge, along with 500 pounds of valuable supplies.

We found our way around the cracks and had no more misfortunes. By noontime we safely reached the cache and dropped our loads. Returning to the ship with empty sledges, we made good time. When within sight of the Cape, we had a grand race. Ooqueah won; I was last, but not by many yards. I was glad to see the *Roosevelt* again and have a comfortable bed. On my next trip I learned more about the Arctic.

Mr. Mac and a sailor left with two Eskimos and

their wives to survey unexplored areas and measure tides at Cape Columbia. Professor Marvin made studies on shore ice to the east, according to instructions given by the U.S. Coast and Geodetic Survey. He offered to show me how to take the measurements, but he really wanted help. I couldn't refuse. We had to stay there for several days. There wasn't enough oil to heat the tent, and I was cold when trying to sleep.

We cut a hole four feet down through the ice and drove a stake into the bottom of the bay. Mr. Marvin explained, "We measure the tide by how far it lifts the floating ice shelf and the tent above the inches marked on the stake. We have to record our findings every hour—more often at high and low tides."

To my surprise the tides didn't arrive at high and low on a regular schedule, and the average was only 1.8 feet. After the first readings it was a boring job. We took turns—each had a nine-hour watch. It was a lonely time—I missed George and Mr. Mac, and wished Ooqueah had come with me. After Professor Marvin appeared to relieve me, I couldn't sleep at an unusual hour. At the end of my third watch, I stayed to talk to him. I asked if he liked teaching.

"Very much. And the summers give me time to

follow my own interests. I have a leave of absence for this expedition."

"Mr. Peary relies on you a lot, doesn't he?" I asked.

"Well, I'm interested in the logistics of the journey. For twenty-five years the Commander has been solving the problems of Arctic living. He has endured a great deal to learn how to carry enough food and reduce weight. I think this time we've worked out a support system that will get him to the Pole and back. He'll explain that to everyone. Now tell me about you. Do you like school?"

"Not lately," I said. "Being here is more interesting. Matt has taught me a lot and I'm curious about those cliffs in Greenland.

"I can lend you some geology books you might like," he offered. "You'll have plenty of time to read—winter is coming."

I wished he hadn't reminded me that four months of darkness were ahead.

CHAPTER 16

October 1st was the last day we saw the sun. I watched the shadows of the mountains of Greenland and Grant Land stretch to the blue-black northern horizon. Between them a piece of the sun shone out on the polar ice. The wide yellow path glowed, then grew faint and disappeared. It was frightening to know it wouldn't be back for months. For a few weeks the twilight lasted; then by November 1st it was totally dark except for moonlight. I dreaded the winter. We had no connection with the outside world; I hadn't had a letter since we left Labrador.

The Commander tried to keep us all busy. We lived on the ship, except when we were on hunting expeditions or moving supplies by moonlight. We made walls of snow blocks around the deck house and covered the roof with snow, so we were quite comfortable.

I had to get used to a new routine of two meals a day. "I'll starve to death, Charley," I complained.

"No, you won't. I won't let you. I swear you have grown an inch since July. That's why you are hungry."

I found living on two meals wasn't too bad, since I had less exercise. And breakfast was huge— oatmeal and ham and eggs, or sometimes fish or meat stew. Once or twice I raided the galley cupboard for a cup of cocoa and some of Charley's good bread.

The moon shone continuously for eight or ten days, helping to relieve the gloom. It turned the snow into shining silver, like a fairyland. Because of it, we saw few northern lights, and they were not as bright as those at home. Between moons, the stars were very bright, and I learned the Inuit names and stories for constellations.

Pointing to the Big Dipper, Ooqueah said, "Herd of deer." When I pointed to the Pleiades he said, "Dogs chasing polar bear." The bright stars in Orion's belt were "three steps in a glacier to help a tired traveler." Some "nights" I walked out to look at the bright stars and make up my own stories. I thought a lot about dogs and other animals.

Once some Eskimos brought in Arctic hares in their snow-white winter coats. "Isn't it hard to see white animals in the moonlight?" I asked.

Ooqueah explained. "We see their shadows." He was enjoying winter life because everything was provided for him. He could live aboard ship, have plenty to eat and go hunting.

Before the end of the month the Commander put up a notice saying that Thursday, November 26, 1908, was proclaimed Thanksgiving Day. I looked forward to any kind of celebration, but I couldn't help thinking of the last one I had celebrated with my father and cousins in New York. I was sad, remembering that I would never have one like that again. I missed Aunt Bessie and wondered if she would be cooking a turkey this year.

On the holiday everyone was back at the ship, and Charley and I served musk ox steaks, bread, and mince pie. I saved a steak for Ooqueah and handed it to him later with a knife and fork, which he had never used. He was so careful with the fork it looked as if he were afraid he would puncture his mouth, but he good-naturedly kept using it.

In the afternoon the crew started having fun boxing. They tried unsuccessfully to teach the Eskimos, but they didn't like getting hit and went outside to play football in the moonlight. Their ball was a hide stuffed with hair, relatively soft. They played with two teams in lines facing each other, each trying to kick the ball through the other line and to a goal. It never rose over their heads. I brought out my football and kicked it down the shore to George. When they saw it sailing through the air, they yelled in excitement and scrambled after it. George threw a long pass back to me, and soon I had a crowd around me, wanting to touch it.

"What makes it so hard?" Ooqueah asked, pounding it with his fist. He didn't believe it was air inside. I showed him how to pass and kick. The other Eskimos wrestled to get a chance to play with it. I wished I had brought more than one ball. I had seen them entertaining themselves with dances, songs and story-telling, but they seemed to like athletic games best.

Early in December the Commander sent Matt and Mr. Marvin out in the moonlight to teach the new assistants and me how to build igloos. Matt poked in the snow with a sharp pole to find some firm enough. "Cut some two-foot-long blocks," he directed, and we did so with our saw knives, which had a sharp knife on one side and a saw on the other. We cut about fifty blocks, about 24 by

18 by 6 inches, and placed them around a circular line that Seegloo drew in the snow. Leaving a tiny entrance hole, we built them up, leaning them toward the center and bonding the edges together. We had to work on the inside. It was exciting to see the walls rise and make smaller and smaller circles.

When there was only a small opening in the top, Matt said, "Close it with one block." I shoved the narrow end through the hole, carved the ends and lowered the block. We stuffed snow in the cracks around it. Out of more blocks we built a sleeping platform, and in front of it Seegloo and I dug the floor down a foot, to make standing and cooking space. Near the entrance we made two small shelves to hold the stoves.

When Seegloo put another block in the entrance, Matt lit a lamp. As the walls began to drip, I was puzzled. How long before they would melt? Right away, Matt made a four-inch hole in the top block. As the cold air came in, it formed an icy wall, and soon our ice dome began to glisten like glass. Wonderful! To close the hole, Matt stuffed his mitt in it.

We were working in our lighter sheepskin jackets. Seegloo took his "til-lug-tuk" (pronounced til-luck-too), a short heavy stick, and beat the snow out of our furs that we would put on again at night—he didn't want heat from the stoves to melt the snow and wet them. Matt lit the wicks of both little nine-inch-high alcohol stoves and put on the cans of ice to melt, turning back the lid of the kitchen box to keep the heat from melting the wall. We dried our socks on a snowshoe that he stuck into the wall of the igloo a foot above the stove.

I sat on the platform, with my feet in the lower area—it was more comfortable than squatting in a tent. At last I knew how to build an igloo. I hoped to have a chance to help build another.

Matt and the Captain kept the trails west open all winter, and built permanent igloos with tunnel entrances. They hauled most of the loads from the caches to Cape Columbia. I made two more trips to caches, in moonlight, with a lantern along. I liked being busy, and it was a good feeling to know I had helped a little with the mammoth task of hauling twenty thousand pounds of food and equipment.

My traveling companions were constantly teaching me. When we stopped for the dogs to rest, like Panikpah and Ooqueah I stuck my nose over the top of the lantern chimney to warm it. Another thing I learned from them was to look over my clothes each morning for rips and mend them. I didn't want to get frostbite.

Returning to the ship, I was always glad to see the yellow gleam of the galley lamp shining through the window, piercing the darkness.

George was busier than I and always happy—he loved to hunt, but could only do it in moonlight. He and the Eskimos with him came in with a polar bear, a rare animal this far north. Its upper legs were bigger than two of mine, and its huge paws were a foot wide.

"A swipe with those could crush your head like an eggshell," George said. I believed him. I watched the men skin it, and later enjoyed a juicy steak.

George was our photographer. The scientists wanted nude pictures of the body structure of the Eskimos to show doctors and anthropologists at home. The Eskimos didn't seem to mind modeling, and I knew how curious people at home were about this isolated tribe. In the low temperature George had his problems keeping the camera lens free of moisture. He held his breath while the light was burning, and told the Eskimos "Don't breathe for the minute it takes to get the picture, or it will look like a cloud in front of your face."

Sometimes the gas in the lamp he used for printing leaked and exploded, frightening his models. We called it "Borup's Blow-up Lamp." The children hauled water for his developing machine from the lake, making several trips. One evening he was developing pictures with a red lantern for dim light. Suddenly Harrigan came screaming out of the room and ran off across the ice as though the devil was after him.

When George came out, laughing, I asked, "What happened?"

"Oh, I really scared the poor devil. I threw in the developing fluid and acted like a magician waving a magic wand. When he saw his own face appearing with the blacks and whites reversed, he went piblocto."

"George, you're mean," I told him. After that, we called his developing room "The Chamber of Horrors."

CHAPTER 17

The Commander stayed on the ship most of the winter, planning in detail for his final effort. To avoid monotony and depression among the staff, he tried to keep our minds and hands occupied making sledge parts. He had brought plenty of rough wood. I welcomed the jobs, but there were times when I longed for daylight. I hated the darkness—the thickness of it, the heaviness, the monotony of getting up and going to bed by lamplight.

The dark days were hardest to bear when storms kept me in. Gales from the south became more violent. During these storms and times of intense cold, I wanted to hide from the screaming wind, but there was no escape. It creaked in the rigging and howled around the deck house as though it were angry at our presence. I understood why the Eskimos believed in evil spirits and devils.

119

I thought often of my father and what he had endured on the sea ice. Even so, I wanted to get out there just a short way to help the Commander reach the Pole. The promise of it would get me through the rest of the winter. I was strong enough and had learned to handle a dog team almost as well as George, so I dared to hope I might be asked.

The dogs began to worry us because recent hunting parties had had no luck and supplies of meat were seriously low. Several had died, and many were in poor condition. Some of them developed piblocto, the Inuit word for a form of hydrophobia.

"Is it catching?" I asked Matt.

"No, but the husky howls and snaps and won't eat. There have been five cases, and the dogs had to be shot."

"How many healthy dogs are left?"

"A hundred ninety-three out of the 246," he replied. "But the whale meat doesn't seem to be nutritious. Four in the worst condition were killed to save dog food."

The report was horrifying—I felt sick. "What are you feeding them now?" I asked.

"The Commander's going to try pork."

I began to wonder if there would be enough dogs left for the spring journey to the Pole.

On December 21st, the day before the winter solstice, the temperature dropped to 53 below, the coldest recorded yet at the ship. To cheer us, the Commander planned a celebration. He called everyone on deck and at four o'clock he announced, "The sun has started back toward us. We're half way through the darkness."

Professor Marvin rang the ship's bells, and Matt fired three shots from a revolver. When George set off a bunch of flashes, everyone cheered. Afterwards, we went to the galley and mess-room to have musk ox steaks, biscuits and coffee. The announcement helped me believe I would survive the rest of the winter.

One of the few times we were all together was at Christmas, and we celebrated in great style. We all wore clean flannel shirts and neckties, Charley wore a chef's hat, and I laid the table with a linen cloth and our best silver. Before dinner we enjoyed some merry music played on the pianola; then Christmas packages that had been put aboard last July were brought out. Mrs. Peary had sent gifts of sweets for everyone. I opened my gift from Aunt Bessie.

"What did she send you?" Mr. Mac asked.

"Warm socks, a book, tooth powder and some candy. Wouldn't she be surprised to see the 'socks' I'm wearing!"

Charley and I cooked up a wonderful meal, with musk ox meat, sponge cake, chocolate, and even plum pudding, but it seemed strange without family and a tree. I thought of the last Christmas I had with my father, when he promised me another camping trip. I wished he knew the sort of camping trip I took!

Later the Captain, Mr. Mac and George laid out a track, lined it with lamps and held races for everyone. It seemed warm compared to a few days before—it was only 23 below.

"Women's races first," the Captain shouted. "Line up." Even the mothers with babies on their backs raced 50 yards. They ran, but not fast, and the babies didn't seem to mind bouncing. Men winners chose food for prizes; the women and girls liked the sewing kits of needles, thread and thimbles. The final event was a tug of war—the sailors beat the assistants. After all the exercise, I slept well.

In January a wide-ranging storm kept us in for two days, and when it suddenly got warmer, I came down with the grippe. So did Dr. Goodsell, and some of the Eskimos and crew were ill, too. The

Doctor said the wind had brought us germs from the south. We had fever and sore throats, and I ached all over. I was in bed for almost two weeks, and with the Doctor sick and no hospital available, I couldn't help being scared. Even though I couldn't mail it, I wrote a letter to my aunt—it made me feel closer to home—but I didn't tell her how sick I was. I remembered the times she had nursed me through illnesses. The expedition would be starting in a month, and I was lying in bed getting weaker every day. I cursed my luck. Would I be well and strong enough to take part in the work in February?

One night the sound of the ship groaning woke me. I had heard that frightening sound before—pressure from the ice. I was still awake in the middle of the night when the Captain shouted, "All hands on deck! The ice is coming for us!"

I staggered out of bed. The ice growled even louder and the ship creaked and groaned. Men, women and children were abandoning ship. Charley and I followed the crowd to the box houses. The ice in the channel outside broke with a roar and started to pile up behind the berg that was protecting the ship's stern. The ridge was thirty feet high and getting bigger. The Commander was out there with a lantern to see if there was any damage. I feared for his safety.

The ship listed a little to port. Charley looked really worried. "If she's pushed over on her side our galley stove could start a fire." That was always our worst nightmare.

"The tide turns in another hour. Maybe that will remove the pressure," I said hopefully. We watched for two hours. The ship seemed to tilt a little more, but in time the tide did move the ridge away, and we found that she was not seriously damaged. Shivering, I went gratefully back to bed. The Doctor and I and all the patients were slowly recovering.

The Commander planned to start for the Pole as early as possible, in the cold twilight period late in February. I was invited to a meeting in the mess room when he carefully explained to the staff his method of using support parties on the trip from the Cape to the Pole.

"The biggest problem is transporting enough food and fuel. I can't carry enough to go to the Pole and back, and it's no use to leave caches of supplies on the trail. Crossing moving sea ice is not like traveling on land—I would never be sure of finding them because the pack ice moves. It's up to the supporting parties to get enough supplies to us when we are closer to the Pole. A pioneer group will make a trail each day and build two igloos at the end of the march. Each of you will follow in your turn, with two Eskimos and three sledges. You'll go on until you hand over your supplies to other divisions, to replace what has been used. Then you will be sent back." He illustrated this for the Eskimos by using matches to represent sledges.

"You young assistants will make it possible for the advance party to go on with full loads. If a spring thaw slows my return, I'll have enough food and alcohol with me to wait it out." The Commander looked around the room. As he said solemnly, "That's your job," I thought he was looking at me. "How far you go depends on time and your condition. Some of you will take the weakest dogs home. You will keep the trail open—that will make traveling easier and quicker for me when I return. The final advance party will consist of the best drivers and dogs, with plenty of provisions."

He paused, then said, "I depend on you to make it possible for me to get to the Pole and back." My skin tingled all over my back and arms, and I prayed

I would be able to help this dedicated man. I worked hard daily to get back in shape.

From then on there was great activity aboard. The Doctor arranged the medical equipment, and Mr. Mac marked off fathoms on the sounding line. Matt was still working on the new alcohol cookers. I watched them with envy, feeling left out. The Commander was everywhere, restlessly checking details. The assistants seemed confident about what was ahead, and after all their constant activity and practice they were in excellent physical shape. I felt I was in good condition, too.

CHAPTER 18

Early in February at noon a thin band of light appeared in the south—a welcome sight. Each day the twilight grew longer and I could see pale colors and pink and gold clouds in the southern sky. Soon the coming sun was reflected on the snows on the south sides of the high peaks. I had never seen anything like it—it was a riot of color. That was a great lift to my spirits. Then one day I got an even greater one. In the morning of February 15th I was in the galley, slumped over the work shelf, staring at nothing and thinking.

Charley asked, "What are you moping about?"

I hesitated, then answered, "This is the day my father died a year ago."

Charley came over to me, put his big hand on my back and said, "He was a fine man. He'd be proud of you."

"But I want so much to do more." All I could

think of was Father's dream. I was listless until later in the day, when Mr. Peary came in and surprised me. "Henson tells me you can handle a sledge well. You're a strong young man, and I've decided to let you go a short way on the sea ice, if you stay with Doctor Goodsell. I'll send Ooqueah with you—he's one of the best. They'll keep you out of trouble, and I'll be behind you. Are you game for two or three marches? We could use your muscle."

I had been praying this would happen; nevertheless I was startled by the suddenness. I could hardly get the words out. "Y—es, Sir, Mr. Peary. I was hoping to do that."

He shook my hand and said, "Good. We'll soon be on our way."

When he had gone I yelled to the black skies. This was what I had dreamed about. Charley smiled to see my excitement.

"Did you hear that?" I asked.

"I told you your father would be proud of you. You've earned it."

Then I wondered, "Why did the Commander tell me today?" Had he remembered the date and done it as a kindness? It seemed like a memorial to Father, and I resolved to do my best.

When the big day came, we got ready for the final trip from the ship. The men shaved off their hair, and Mr. Mac shaved me bald, too. We all took hot baths in our barrel tubs. Mr. Peary's would be his last for almost three months. He had over a thousand miles to go to the Pole and back. Matt had rearranged teams to give each of us eight or more dogs, and again I had Karko with me.

The Captain and Matt left, followed by four other divisions on different days. I was in Dr. Goodsell's. We hoped to do the 93 mile route to the Cape in four marches and meet the other divisions there. Leaving the ship was different this time—I didn't know how long it would be before I returned. I looked back for a moment at the ship, waved to Charley, then turned to the west.

The trail was smoother by now, and igloos had already been built. We did two long marches of 25 miles each. On the third, tall cliffs appeared, and we had to go out around many dark headlands. When a storm stopped us, we took shelter at the base of a cliff, cowering behind a large rock while the gale howled around us. Suddenly we jumped in alarm as we heard sounds like explosions only a few feet away. I was terrified, and flattened my back against the rock wall. The Doctor's eyes were wider than I had ever seen them. What was happening?

We realized the wind had picked up huge boulders and blown them over the edge of the precipice to crash into pieces in front of us. When we recovered somewhat from our fright, the Doctor scowled at the fragments near us. "I bet those boulders weighed over a hundred pounds. Thank heaven we weren't out in that wind." I agreed, but I didn't like it where I was, either. Even though cold and hungry, we didn't risk moving from under the cliff until the gale stopped.

I was thankful to be alive to see the twin peaks at Cape Columbia on the fifth day. Mr. Mac had taken five days, too. We were now at 83 degrees 7 minutes north, 70 degrees west longitude, 413 nautical miles from the Pole. The camp looked like a village, igloos nestled closely together at the base of a sloping mountain. Seven members of the party, fourteen Eskimos, 133 dogs, nineteen sledges and mounds of supplies were gathered at the Cape, waiting for Mr. Peary to arrive.

My breath had made crystals on the fur around my face, and my nose and cheeks felt frozen. Ooqueah warmed them with his hand, and the Doctor put drops in my eyes to relieve the pain caused by the wind. The toes on my right foot were numb. Sipsu, one of our helpers, offered to warm them under his bearskin jacket, against his warm body. That felt *so* good. After a few minutes I realized he expected me to do the same for him. When he uncovered two very dirty feet, I was a bit startled but lifted my kooletah. When they touched the skin of my stomach I gasped and couldn't help squirming—it was like hugging a piece of ice, and it took some time for his feet to warm.

I helped Ooqueah and Panikpah repair the igloo we were to eat and sleep in with the Doctor. Then I watched Matt repairing tins of alcohol that had been punctured by jolting on the sledge. If he took his mitts off, his fingers soon froze; if he tried to solder with them on, the mitts burned. Somehow he got the job done. This man could do anything required of him—no wonder the Commander said he couldn't get along without him.

My respect for Matt continued to grow. I wished that Mr. Peary could treat him as a friend. And the Eskimos were like servants, too. I told Matt, "They are as patient as you are in taking orders constantly, yet we kill their dogs, and Ooqueqah tells me hunting is getting harder and seals are scarce. We are driving their musk ox herds inland, but they don't complain."

"Do you know that about ten years ago scientists asked Mr. Peary to bring some of them to New York?"

"No, did he?" I asked.

"Yes, he took a man and his son, and another man with his wife and daughter and the man who was planning to be her husband. You've seen the American Museum of Natural History, haven't you?" When I nodded, he continued, "The families were cared for in the basement."

I was almost afraid to ask. "What happened to them?"

"They all got sick—couldn't stand the heat—and four died of pneumonia. One was adopted, and Mr. Peary brought the sixth back to Greenland."

I was too shocked to say anything, but I was remembering Father's comments about the damage sometimes done to native people by the pride and power of the white man.

Matt said, "But don't think the Eskimos are unhappy now. They think there's no one like Mr. Peary. He has done so much for them for years—he brought them wood and guns and tools, and has often saved them from starving."

As he put away the repaired tins he said, "Two Eskimos aren't fit to go on the ice —torn muscles—and six dogs in one team died from throat distemper. That changes the divisions, and I'll have to rearrange teams." It seemed he no sooner finished one job than another was waiting for him.

On the afternoon of February 26th we heard yells, and the dogs set up a howl. Three sledges and teams raced down the slope toward the camp, snow dust flying around them. In the lead, in new furs and a red skull cap, was Mr. Peary, followed by Ootah and Egingwah. The Commander had shaved off his long mustache—it would only collect ice. He looked younger. We gave rousing cheers to welcome him, and everyone talked excitedly.

That night was the coldest yet. Even the Eskimos shivered, but it didn't bother the dogs. The four assistants and I gathered in one igloo and started a fire to dry our mitts and kamiks. We couldn't get warm, and sat up all night drinking hot tea, while the dogs gave us a concert outside. When I heard 180 of them joyfully baying—well, it was comical, and I've never forgotten it. I wondered what they were saying to one another.

Inside, the men competed by singing college songs. I noticed their voices were not as light-hearted as usual. They were feeling, as I was, the seriousness of what was ahead. They all pledged to watch out for the Commander and get him to the Pole at any cost—loss of hands or feet, or their

133

lives. What loyalty! I prayed that I could meet the unknown challenge ahead. While the temperature dropped to 57 below, the moaning of the wind, a sudden roar of the ice, then sounds like thunder kept me awake. I wondered how far I would get toward the Pole.

Mary Irwin

CHAPTER 19

In the morning the Eskimos became upset, fearing Tornarsuk, the Devil, blaming him for the strong east wind that was blowing. The Commander said that was the first time in his experience it had come from that direction, but he would not delay—he wanted to reach the area of the Big Lead before it became as wide as on the last trip. He sent Captain Bartlett and George, with three Eskimos, to scout and open a trail. Matt was to follow their trail the next day, then Professor Marvin, Mr. Mac, and the doctor, each with two Eskimos and three sledges. The Commander would come last, with Egingwah, a big Eskimo of about 175 pounds, who had been his driver two years ago.

Each division was self-sufficient. Every driver carried 500 pounds of dog pemmican, 50 pounds for the men, tea and condensed milk, biscuits, alcohol and a stove. We all had snowshoes, extra boots and mittens, pickaxes and spades, ice lances and saw knives for cutting snow blocks, and a kit for mending sledges. The Commander would carry the sextant, and materials to make an artificial horizon. I had asked Professor Marvin what that meant, and he explained, "The sun will be so low he has to pour mercury into a flat iron pan and use the reflection of the sun to figure his position. You will probably get a chance to see that." I hoped I would.

My division had to wait the longest. After Matt, the Professor and Mr. Mac had left with their divisions, I stood with my back to the wind in the morning twilight, waiting impatiently for the signal from Mr. Peary. The Commander gave us final instructions. His orders to me were, "Go with the Doctor and stay with him and Ooqueah. Keep them in sight." This was far more exciting than waiting to be called off the bench in a game, but once the order came I wasn't nervous any more.

Dr. Goodsell led off; Ooqueah and I followed. The gale blew sharp ice crystals into my face, but I kept up with Ooqueah. Within an hour ridges loomed up ahead, much bigger than they had looked from the ship. Some of the floating pack ice had cracked open, and huge pieces were driven by currents and the wind to smash against the shelf ice, pushing up snow-covered hills—some fifty to sixty feet high.

"Are we going over *those?*" I asked Ooqueah in disbelief.

Mary Irwin

"Yes, but slowly," he said. "You'll see." Ooqueah had had practice on the Commander's last trip.

The ice was quiet at the moment, but now I could understand the sounds like earthquakes that I had often heard. I stared at the mountainous ridges in wonder. When we came closer I could see trails the assistants ahead of us had carved around and over the ice peaks, but they looked very rough.

When the dogs couldn't pull the sledges, it took all three of us to haul them one at a time up the hills. To brace them and keep them from sliding back down, we had to dig in our toes. While we worked on one sledge, the other dogs, quiet for once, slept curled up in the snow, noses in their tails.

The march was like climbing mountains—you got up one and there was another one beyond. Sometimes the mound was so steep we had to unpack loads; then on the way down the hill we held the sledges back so the dogs would not be overrun. It was hard work, and I was perspiring, even in the cold wind. I loosened my kooletah and the air vents in my pants.

Ooqueah said, "You are strong, like Inuit."

I took it as a great compliment and was thankful I could do my share.

The next ridge was lower. After successfully

pushing up it, I became worried when I started down the other side. I yelled to Ooqueah as the sledge threatened to overrun the dogs. To slow it, I dug my heels in and leaned all the way backward. About a gallon of snow came up inside my loosened kooletah. Doggone! That was icy cold against my stomach.

At the same time I heard a thud and an awful smashing sound—the sledge had rammed an icy mound and flipped over. The dogs stopped yelping and sat on their haunches. I shook the snow off my stomach and Ooqueah helped me turn the sledge over. To my dismay, it was cracked and one upstander was busted. I slumped at the foot of the hill and stared gloomily at the broken handle. Ooqueah didn't say anything—he just got out the mending kit.

The Doctor waited for us. "Cheer up, Tom," he said. "I'm sure there will be a dozen others before we get over these ridges." I felt less discouraged having a partner like him.

Repairing the sledge meant unloading it, undoing the lashings, and boring new holes with the brace and bit. To thread the sealskin thongs through the holes I had to take my gloves off, and when I finished, my fingers felt frozen. I pulled my arms out of my sleeves and warmed my icy fingers under my armpits. When I felt them burning, I knew they were thawed.

As I worked, Ooblooyah, who had been ahead of us with Mr. Mac, appeared over a ridge with his team of dogs. His sledge was so badly broken that he had left it and his load, and was returning for another.

When mine was mended, we pushed on. My body ached all over. The twilight was gone when we reached the first camp ten miles out. Ooqueah carried pemmican tins, the alcohol stove and the tiny oil burner with a two-inch wick we used for drying mittens into the camp. We had no heat and could do no cooking now, only make tea. We were cold, but thirst was a greater problem.

I crawled in, filled the tin boilers with ice, and poured alcohol into the small but efficient Peary stove, which would melt the ice and provide a gallon of hot water in ten minutes. Our lives depended on hot tea. When I lit a match nothing happened— it was so cold the fuel wouldn't vaporize. I froze with panic, and Ooqueah's hand trembled with fright. "Tornarsuk angry," he said.

The Doctor said, "Try this." He lit some paper and dropped it into the alcohol. It ignited. I started to breathe again. While we waited, I chopped the pemmican tins into one-pound sections—one from

a red tin for each dog, a blue one for each man—
and took out the eight sea biscuits I was allowed.
When the water was hot, I used half a can of frozen condensed milk for my quart of tea, thankful
that I didn't have to drink cold water. The hot
drink warmed my insides, but the frozen pemmican hurt my mouth. I tried warming it in my tea
but it didn't improve the taste. At least it was better than Ahnalka's preserved auks.

Everything in the igloo was covered with our
frozen breath, and the frost cemented my eyelashes
together. I kept beating my arms and legs to keep
the circulation going. Ooqueah saw me rubbing
my cold feet. He offered to warm them in the usual
way. I was relieved that they weren't seriously frost-
bitten. I threw down a piece of fur to lie on, fully
clothed, and tried to close my ears to the rumble
of pack ice in the distance. The sounds did seem
like warnings.

In the morning the gale was still blowing. "Only
Peary would travel in this weather," the Doctor
grumbled. "The wind sounds like a pack of
wolves."

Before we left the camp I emptied my bowels
into a tin inside the igloo, to have protection from

the wind and the dogs. I had seen Eskimos huddle in a circle on the ice, facing out, or with someone nearby with a whip to keep the dogs away from their stools until they had finished. I preferred to make it to shelters, out of the cold wind.

When I went out, facing the gale was like trying to move a wall. Pushing my way up a football field against human interference was child's play compared to this. My eyes stung and my cheeks were burning. Before long my knees ached, and I began to think there really was some inhuman sea devil spirit trying to guard the way north.

CHAPTER 20

I thought of Tornarsuk again when we came to a crack in the floating ice. The lead across our path extended out of sight east and west. The Doctor stared at it. "Too wide to risk having the dogs jump this," he said gloomily. "But we can't wait for the wind to close it. Let's try the bridge the Commander described—the ice is thick on each side."

We unloaded my sledge and unhitched the dogs' traces from it. Ooqueah and Panikpah held the team while I pushed the sledge forward until it spanned the crack. "Climb over," the Doctor said.

I scrambled over, trying to keep the sledge steady. When I reached the far side, he dragged my lead dog to the end of the sledge. It braced its legs—he had to use his whip to make the animal cross over. One at a time he sent me the rest of my team, dragging their traces, which I fastened to the toggle on the front of the sledge. Ooqueah replaced the load, and the dogs pulled it over the gap. After the Doctor and Ooqueah sent their dogs and loaded sledges, I pushed an empty sledge back over the gap so they could join me. I was relieved when we were together again.

"Good trick," Ooqueah commented. It was unusual that we had been able to teach an Inuit something about sledge travel.

At the end of the march I was ready for a rest, but it was so cold that night we couldn't sleep soundly. I wondered if I shivered enough would it make me warmer? I thought of the warm days back at Etah, with flowers blooming, and that made me more miserable. This weather was the coldest yet.

Ooqueah suggested, "Build the sleeping platform up higher, close to the top."

That helped. Later, when I read the thermometer, I couldn't believe it. "It's up to 40 below!" I shouted. "That's 25 degrees warmer than at the lower floor."

With my head pillowed on the snow, the cracking of the ice around us sounded like explosions. When I finally slept, I dreamed about Father. It seemed like a short time until the Doctor woke me, but it was late, and after a quick breakfast we started out. To my relief, the wind had died and the air was clearer. The sky was getting lighter each day, and it was easier now to locate the trail by spotting Bartlett's marker—an empty tin fastened to a peak of ice.

This was my sixteenth birthday, but I hadn't told anyone except George. Everyone was too exhausted to think about celebrations. What would the day be like? Surely far different from any I had had before, and one I would remember.

Around noon we had been traveling in twilight, as usual, with the southern sky turning bright pink. Suddenly Ooqueah shouted, "Suck-in-nuck! Suck-in-nuck!" (The sun! The sun!)

I turned to see the tip of the red sun showing between the mountains. It was beautiful. It was dazzling. The sky turned from gray to blue. Ooqueah and Panikpah took their mitts off and held their bare hands high to greet the sun and give thanks that they were still alive. I squinted and yelled, as all in the party cheered. It had been months since we had seen the sun. We stood around looking at it for a few more seconds before it was gone again. It was the best birthday present I could possibly have, and we would see it for a longer time each day from now on.

As we moved ahead I felt lucky to be where I was, and for the first time in my life to see the return of the sun after more than four months. What a day! It made up for all the aches and pains and worry about freezing. I went on, with new energy.

When we came to the igloos, I left the loaded sledge, unhitched the dogs and tied them to an ice anchor nearby. The ice rumbled, then I jumped as I heard a loud report and cracking sounds. As it started to move, I stood still, stiff with fright. The dogs cowered, and I heard Ooqueah shout "Takoo!" (Look!)

I looked back and groaned at what I saw. The igloo was in shambles, and my sledge was now perched on the side of a ridge of broken ice. Some of the contents had spilled out in spite of the lashings, and several tins of alcohol and food teetered over a crack that was opening under them.

"Oh no! Tornarsuk, you devil, you can't have them!" I shouted. I had worked so hard to get them this far—they mustn't be lost. I grabbed my pickax, climbed the ridge and threw the tins down to Ooqueah. Then I started digging out others, all the while keeping an eye on the crack.

"Tom, get off that!" the Doctor yelled. I lowered the last tin off the mound, shoved the sledge down and jumped the crack. The ice at the edge broke, and my left leg went in the water half way up my thigh. Lunging forward, I crawled to safety just as a sound like a rifle shot scared the wits out of me. The dogs were terrified, too, and trembling. The ridge I had been standing on was pushed over by another wall of ice.

"You jumped just in time," the Doctor said, pulling me away.

I moved the dogs, and soon the ice was quiet. I was thankful that my kamiks and pants were tied so tight that no water got in. Not like the last time I took a cold bath at Etah. When ice formed on the outside, I scraped it off. Then I realized how risky my rescue attempt had been—I could easily have had a total dunking, or had a leg crushed. I was very lucky.

The dogs set up a howl, and we saw that Mr. Peary and Egingwah were catching up to us. When they arrived the Doctor said, "We lost an igloo, but Tom rescued your alcohol and food."

The Commander stared at what was left of the igloo and the rescued supplies piled on the ice, then whistled in amazement. When he had inspected the damage, he said, "Some tins are leaking and we lost some alcohol, but you saved most of them. I'm grateful." Looking at my icy pants he said, "But don't take any more risks."

His smile and thanks reassured me. By the time

we built new igloos it had seemed like a long day. I wondered if I would be sent back in the morning.

But when the Commander woke me he asked, "How do you feel?"

"Like doing another march," I said, even though I was tired.

To my surprise he said, "Load up, then, and we'll go on."

I loaded my sledge so fast I was ready before the Doctor was. The traveling was rough. At noon the Commander walked toward a high pinnacle, which he climbed to see what the ice looked like ahead. He soon reported that he had seen a broad band of dark clouds ten miles to the north. "That means open water," he growled. He sent us on our way and followed slowly.

In the afternoon we met George, waiting for us. "All of the divisions are stopped three miles ahead," he reported. "One of our sledges was smashed and one of Mr. Mac's slightly damaged." That was not good news, but it made me feel less guilty about my accident. Smiling mischievously, George took me over to his sledge and handed me a huge birthday cake he had carved out of frozen snow. In the middle he had made the number 16 out of dried dog droppings. "It was the only thing I could find on the way that wasn't white," he said, smirking.

I laughed until my lungs ached from the cold air. "You clown! I'll never forget *this* cake," I gasped. Good old George—he could always think of some fun. And he had remembered and come back to meet me.

When we overtook the Captain and the other divisions camped by a large stretch of open water, I was surprised to see that it was half a mile wide. How long would we be delayed? Each day would use up more supplies. Would the Commander send someone back for more? I learned that several dogs had died of piblocto—that was another discouraging situation. As we built more igloos, I could only think about my chances of going on. Would I be needed or not?

The temperature rose to 20 below, and the air was still for a change. Two Eskimos were making a sledge from a couple of broken ones. I could still see land to the south, but ahead no landmarks broke the monotonous horizon and there were no shadows to mark depressions. The sky was gray. The scene was as strange to me as seeing a tall tree would be for Ooqueah.

When the Commander caught up to us, he glared at the black water and groaned, "That devil, it's big as the Hudson River again." Rough travelling had caused leaks in some of the fuel tanks, and he was worried about the supply. He sent Professor Marvin back with George to bring another load of food, fuel, and fresh dogs. Matt went east and the Captain went west, looking for a place to cross, while the rest of us waited nervously. We began to call the lead the Styx.

CHAPTER 21

The next morning two Eskimos pretended sickness and wanted to return to land. We had all been worried about this—we knew they were terrified to be on the shifting sea ice. The Commander was annoyed and told them to leave the ship when they got back and go home to Etah. When others wanted to go, he got angry and shouted, "No! You are *not* leaving."

Waiting days for ice to form was hard for everyone. Would the Big Lead defeat us? Mr. Mac distracted the Inuit by organizing all kinds of athletic competitions, including their favorite strength contests and seal racing—moving forward on their stomachs and elbows. Ooqueah showed me a harder physical test—he told me to lie face down and push up with only hands and feet touching the ground. When he put a mitt on the ice by my hands, I was supposed to put my right arm beside my body, pick

151

up the glove with my teeth and shove myself up again. At the first try I couldn't do it, but when I moved my left arm closer to my knees I succeeded.

Mr. Mac astonished the Eskimos by doing somersaults and turning cartwheels. They stared, murmuring "piblocto." They knew only tests of strength, but liked to play with him—they admired him because he usually won. He offered prizes—things on the ship, like the rudder, spars, the anchor, and even the keel. We all enjoyed the nonsense, and Mr. Peary was grateful to him for keeping the Eskimos amused and distracted from their fears. What a man! He had been dressing his heel, which had frozen. It was in bad shape—the skin would not heal and his kamiks stuck to the loose flesh. In spite of the pain he was always active and cheerful.

At noon when the sun appeared again, the moving figures of the men made long shadows on the snow. Ooqueah and I pranced and watched ours, laughing as they stretched far beyond us. I posed like the Statue of Liberty, and the outline of my torch went out of sight beyond the water.

Matt came to me and said, "Two Eskimos have gone home with one sledge. On new ice we have to lighten our loads, and some of us may make two trips across it. We could use another driver. The Commander suggests you do one more march."

"Yes!" I shouted. I had expected to be sent home—Mr. Peary could not afford to continue feeding all of us. I grabbed Matt's arm and thanked him. He left to explore along the lead.

An hour later a cry "Ice" rang out and was repeated. Matt returned and reported, "I found thin ice to the west, safe enough for us to cross, I think."

We hitched up the teams and went to the spot. A film had formed across a gap of about 100 feet, but I couldn't tell how thick it was, and dreaded finding out if it would support us. Matt led the way. His division spread out, and one at a time started to cross on snowshoes. Waiting for my turn, I took a deep breath to try to stay calm. When I finally let the dogs move forward, my feet felt heavy, as though weighted with lead. The dogs wanted to go faster than I did. Using voice commands, it was hard to keep them from running.

The length of the sledge spread its weight, but the ice ahead of it pushed up in a frozen wave. When I walked behind it, the ice sagged in ripples under me. Unlike rigid ice on lakes, this was like loose skin—it was rubber ice. I took slow steps. Dreading a bath, I held my breath and spread my feet, sliding my snowshoes. Now I understood the reason for having such long ones.

Breathless and trembling, I finally reached firm footing. Miraculously, no one broke through, and we all crossed safely. I was tired, but thankful to be alive. When I remembered how far I had come, I couldn't help grinning. I was well satisfied to be 330 miles from the Pole. My one march beyond the Big Lead helped Mr. Peary to be well supplied if he were delayed on his return.

The Commander had us build more igloos. He paced nervously, waiting for George and Mr. Marvin and the precious alcohol. I heard him say, "As soon as they come, I can go on." I was able to sleep soundly, in spite of all the excitement of the day. This one and my birthday had been special. What a tale I would have to tell!

In the morning I heard a shout from Seegloo, who was standing on top of a hummock. "Kling-mik-sue!" (Dogs are coming.) I climbed up beside him. Sure enough, it was George and Mr. Marvin, with their precious loads of supplies and alcohol. They were over the Big Lead! We were all relieved—the whole encampment turned out to cheer them.

"Found your trail," George said. "You led us to

the new ice. Jerusalem! Was I glad we could get across that devil of a lead." Besides fuel and supplies, he had brought fresh dogs. We hustled up some tea for him and Mr. Marvin.

Now I knew I would be sent back, with some of the Eskimos. I prayed the ice would be frozen solid. I was not surprised to learn that Mr. Mac was returning with Panikpah and me and the weakest dogs. He had counted on going a lot farther, but he was really not fit for more travel because of his heel. I knew how disappointed he must be.

The Captain had gone ahead, and Matt had worked for hours rearranging dogs and loading supplies—heavy loads for those going north and light ones for us. When he made new teams, the dogs fought again for leadership, so there was quite a ruckus for awhile. I said goodbye reluctantly to Mr. Marvin and the Doctor, wishing them success. They shook my hand, thanked me, and said kind things like "Good man. One of us." That made me feel I had done my share of the work.

Ooqueah was to go on. I hated to leave him, but I was thankful to have been his partner. "I'm sure you'll make it," I told him. "You're as good as any of the drivers."

He smiled and said, "Ahpy. (Yes) I am strong." I said goodbye to Karko, gave her a hug and scratched her ears. How far would she go?

I interrupted Matt at his work long enough to wish him good luck and to thank him. "Without your help I'd never have been able to come this far," I said. "I'm very happy."

"You learned fast, Tom, and you've done a good job."

"I had the best possible teacher—I'll never forget what a good friend you have been and all you have taught me." I took his hand and didn't want to let go. "I know you'll make it all the way. The Commander needs you."

"I'll know in about a week," he said. "And I'll see you early in May." He had to get back to work, so I left him, wishing him well with all my heart.

George was needed for a while, too. He was a strong driver. When I said goodbye he pounded me on the back and said, "Keep your feet dry and stay out of trouble. Save me a steak."

It was hard to leave my friends. I tried to sound more cheerful than I felt—I wouldn't know for a long time what was happening to them. Underneath all the happy talk and good luck wishes was a nagging fear. I couldn't help wondering if I would see all of them again.

Matt started north. Mr. Mac got instructions from Mr. Peary about mapping and soundings to be done back on land. With one lighter sledge and tired dogs Mr. Mac, Panikpah and I faced south.

Mr. Peary said, "This north wind will be closing the lead soon. You'll be all right." He shook Mr. Mac's hand and to my surprise slapped me on the back, saying, "Well done, Tom." I thought of my father and wished he could see me now. I was older and a lot stronger than when he last saw me.

As we turned south the distorted image of a fiery crimson sun came above the horizon. We welcomed it again with cheers. When we came to the lead, the wind had begun to close it, and after waiting half an hour we crossed safely. Over the well-worn trail, we could make better time now. There were the same problems that we had on the way north, but we handled them with a lot more confidence this time. Mr. Mac didn't complain, and refused to let his painful heel slow us down. With a light load on the sledge he could ride on it when he wished.

The most frightening event took place where we stopped at the end of the third march.

CHAPTER 22

After a few hours' sleep I woke suddenly. I had felt the igloo shudder. "The ice is moving!" I screamed. I quickly put on my boots, kicked out the snow door and crawled through. Mr. Mac and Panikpah followed me. A few yards from the entrance a crack was widening.

"The dogs! The sledge!" I yelled. They were tied on the other side of the crack. They were awake and looking toward me, as they slowly began to drift away. Quickly I ran toward them. Mr. Mac called, "No, Tom! Don't get separated from us."

But I had already jumped the crack and was rushing to them. Grabbing the axe, with one blow I cut the line to free the dogs from their ice anchor. I had left them attached to the sledge. I had the dogs, but I was still separated from the rest of the party, and visions of what that might mean flashed through my mind. An ominous sound increased my fear—the ice was splitting open wider, revealing black water. Quickly I drove the dogs toward it.

"Hurry!" Mr. Mac shouted. The stretch of water was not too wide for the dogs to jump it safely. Snapping the whip, I urged them forward, praying they would leap. They did, but as the sledge straddled the gap with me aboard, the ice cracked at the back end. The whole load tipped and threatened to sink. I clung to the lashing over the load with one hand and used the whip, shouting "Huk! Huk!" The dogs strained, but could not move the sledge. Should I try to climb over it? No, the front edge might break and we'd lose everything. I snapped the whip again, but the load was at too much of an angle.

Another piece of ice broke off and the sledge tipped more. My grip tightened—I didn't dare move. If the ice in front didn't hold, the sledge would drag the dogs into the water. Mr. Mac was yelling at me. "Hold on! Stay where you are!" He went to the igloo, grabbed a red tin of pemmican and threw it on the ice in front of him. The dogs saw it and leaned toward it. Slowly they pulled the sledge and me forward to safety. Then there was a wild fight as the hungry animals attacked the tin with their teeth and ripped it apart to get the pemmican.

I slumped and let out my breath in relief. I was

shaking. Panikpah came to help me off the sledge. Mr. Mac said, "You dare-devil! That was close."

"You saved us!" I gasped. "How did you think of the pemmican? I was sure the dogs and the sledge were going in."

He grinned at me. "I know you haven't had a bath for a couple of weeks, but I didn't want you to have one out here."

After a quick meal we went on, and in spite of exhaustion kept moving, with short rest periods. The hardest thing for me was when one of the dogs just lay down in his harness and died from exhaustion. Poor, faithful animal. Like so many others he gave his life for Mr. Peary's goal. When Panikpah began to cut it up to feed to the other dogs, I couldn't watch and walked away. Should we have given them more rest on the way? The others were thin, but I hoped we could save them. Without them we would be dead. Then I thought of the dogs going north. How many of them would be sacrificed?

When we went on, even though the ice was moving, we found the trail had not shifted much. It was easy to follow, but crossing the mountains of glacial ice took our last reserves of strength. I began to think of the good food stashed in the igloo village.

As we staggered toward the shore, Panikpah said

with a sigh, "Tigerahshua keeshakoyonni!" (We have arrived at last.) I stumbled into an igloo and found a cache of supplies. The pemmican had given us a healthy diet, but the canned beans and pea soup were a treat.

Unbelievably, the temperature rose to 9 degrees below. It felt warm. I lit the stove to melt ice for more tea, but before it was ready I fell asleep. I was worn out physically and mentally. When I woke the stove was out, and the water had frozen. I lit it and fell asleep again. Suddenly I was awakened by the sound of an explosion. Panikpah had put a frozen can of beans on the stove to thaw.

"I told him to punch a hole in the top," Mr. Mac said. "Guess he thought he knew how to cook." Beans were dripping from the wall of the igloo, and Panikpah, near the stove, was wiping some hurriedly from his hair, a look of astonishment in his eyes. We couldn't help laughing at him. He carried bean snacks in his furs for days.

From this camp we made the journey back to the ship in three days, and with all the rest of the dogs. It was downhill all the way to Cape Columbia, so we took turns riding most of the way.

"Oomiaksoah!" Panikpah shouted when he saw the ship. And there she was, with the familiar light in the galley.

What a royal welcome! Charley came over the side in record time. He gave me a bear hug, and I think there were tears in his eyes.

"I made five marches," I bragged. As soon as we boarded, the crew wanted to hear news of the Commander. When the commotion died down, Charley was full of questions. "Are you OK? Was it bad? Were you scared?"

I answered "Yes" to all of them, and said, "I feel great. I went 85 miles toward the Pole."

"Take off those filthy clothes. I'll heat some water for you. You're tired—you look older."

I had never appreciated a bath so much. When I looked in the mirror I didn't recognize the thin face with bloodshot eyes. And was that the beginning of a mustache on my upper lip? I grinned at the strange face with red eyes and wrinkles around them. I felt older, but I had only been away 18 days. How good the food tasted, even the stewed prunes. I had no pains, but I was glad to be idle for a few days.

Doctor Goodsell soon arrived and enjoyed eating and resting, too. In early April he invited me to go out with him for a few days to explore. "We'll take it easy," he promised. By then I was ready to travel again, and Charley didn't need my help.

The snow was beginning to melt, and the Doctor was eager to collect samples of minerals and plants. We loaded a sledge and took two Eskimos as hunters. As we traveled inland toward the Lake Hazen area, I found out how much he knew about biology and geology. He told me something interesting about everything alive or dead in our path. I made my own collection of stones—they would be a treasure of this trip to take home.

As we walked back to the ship, I hoped there would be news. One or more of the assistants and some Eskimos must have returned. When we reached the box houses, Karko greeted me with a yelp. I ran to her—she was thin, but seemed in pretty good shape otherwise. I was thankful she had been sent back, but who had brought her?

Charley answered our questions. "George arrived while you were away. After a rest he went out hunting."

"Doggone, he never wastes a minute. I wanted to see him."

"And Ooqueah?" I asked.

"He isn't back yet." I was glad to hear that—he might go all the way with the Commander.

"And Professor Marvin?"

Charley's smile changed to a frown. Then he

said in a low voice, "Three Eskimos returned and told us that Professor Marvin drowned. He went ahead of them, and they found his body in a lead."

I was stunned. The news chilled my heart. He had been kind to me and taught me a lot—I would miss him. This was a terrible shock to everyone. I knew Mr. Peary especially would mourn his good friend. Mr. Marvin's death made me realize again that all of us had been on a very dangerous journey, and I prayed for the safety of those still on the ice. Matt and the Captain were still with the Commander, and six Eskimos. The rest had returned.

The next day I was helping Charley in the galley when I heard a shout, then more shouts and some of the crew running toward the rail. Three figures and a sledge were approaching. When I recognized Mr. Bartlett and two Eskimos, I was relieved to see them alive, but I was most happy for Matt and Ooqueah—it meant they had gone on to the Pole.

When the hullabaloo quieted down, the Captain reported, "We broke the world record for Farthest North. Matt, Ootah, Egingwah, Seegloo and Ooqueah are making the final marches with the Commander. They were 133 miles from the Pole when I left, and I reached the 88th parallel before turning back."

Well, when the coach of the team orders you

off the field, you go, but the Captain must have been disappointed at not going all the way. Later I heard him remark, "If Peary doesn't make it, you need me to get you and the ship home." He, too, was shocked by the news about Professor Marvin. The gloom aboard ship ruined his triumphant homecoming.

CHAPTER 23

Mr. Mac's heel was no longer painful. His orders were to take more soundings and to explore and map inlets. He asked me to help him, and Charley let me go. More extensive field work was being done on this expedition than ever before—for 90 miles in all directions from the ship. We covered 60 miles and were busy for a week. I often wondered what was happening to the north.

The mapping was more fun than taking soundings. After Mr. Mac approved of my work, I got some good advice from him. "You have a lot of possibilities ahead of you, Tom. I suppose you're going to finish school; I'd like to help you if I can. Would you like to come to Worcester Academy?"

I said, "Gee, Mr. Mac, my grades aren't good enough."

"But you're smart, and I'd recommend you. I think we could arrange a scholarship, if that would help." Then he sat on the platform in our igloo and said in a quiet voice, "I know what it's been like for you, Tom. My father was a sea captain. He sailed away from Provincetown for Labrador, and I never saw him again or heard what happened to him. My mother died the next year."

Hearing that made me feel closer to him—another man besides Matt who understood how I felt. He continued, saying, "I was one of four children and very lucky to be able to go to college."

"How did you manage that?" I asked.

"I worked hard," he answered. "I was janitor at my high school. Late at night I cut linings in the shoe factory, and early in the morning I delivered milk. In the summers I worked at hotels in the White Mountains. Then while I was a student at Bowdoin College I was assistant instructor in gymnastics."

At the look of admiration on my face he grinned, then said, "I'd like to keep an eye on you, if you wouldn't mind."

"No, sir. I wouldn't mind. I'd like that." I was so surprised and grateful that he understood and that he shared his story with me that I didn't know how to thank him. I asked him a lot of questions about the academy. It offered more courses than my school, and it gave me something to think about.

When we returned on April 30th and came in

sight of the ship, we yelled with excitement. The North Pole flag fluttered on the mast and all the international code flags were flying in the rigging. What a thrilling sight! "They made it!" I shouted. "How could they have come back so fast?"

The Captain reported, "Egingwah brought the Commander in two days ago, and Matt, Ooqueah and Ootah arrived yesterday."

What welcome news! And everyone was safe. I climbed aboard to find Ooqueah, and shouted to him, "I'm so glad to see you alive!" He was thinner, but he said, "The devil is asleep or we not come back so easily." Later he commented, "Why go so far to see North Pole? It looks the same as every other place. No nail like the one in the globe on the ship."

When I found Matt, he was smiling sleepily. I was shocked—he had lost 35 pounds and looked older. I grabbed his arm and said, "Oh, Matt, you are safe. And you've won for all of us."

In an exhausted voice, but with quiet pride, he said, "Yes, Tom, on April 6th I held the American flag at the North Pole."

Goose bumps crawled up my arms and back. What must it have been like to stand at the place so many had tried to reach? "What were you thinking then?" I asked.

He grinned slowly. "I was thinking the world

has been waiting for this a long time, and we've made it." After a pause he added, "Mostly I was wondering if we were going to get back."

I let him go back to sleep. For three weeks he was idle, resting and eating, and mourning his friend, Marvin.

George was on board, too. I brought him a specially good lunch, and listened to him brag a little. "I did more hauling than anyone, and I got to within 277 miles of the Pole."

"You don't have to tell *me* how strong you are," I said, congratulating him.

I seldom saw the Commander. He was lean and gaunt, but smiling. Still planning for possible land travel if the ship was lost, he ordered Matt to repair sledges. In May and June we kept on with scientific work. The weather was warm, but fickle. On June 22 it snowed all night, and then it was warm again. We could use tents, and I was thankful for the change—no more drips from melting ice. We were all impatient, waiting for the ice to break up in the channel.

Ooqueah and I toted crates back to the ship. My arms and legs felt strong again. As we returned for another load, I noticed my friend watching me. He laughed and said, "You learned to walk like an Inuit." After a pause he added,

"And you don't shout at me now."

He was right. My life had improved. As I thought about it later, maybe it was because of all I had learned and accomplished on this expedition. I could see ahead. Now I didn't have so much to be angry about.

We hauled all the stores back on board, and the crew put fresh water in the boilers. The icebergs protecting the *Roosevelt* were melting and floating off, and Mr. Peary used dynamite to blow the ice off the propeller. This time I kept on working without worrying about the explosions.

On July 7th we started south. The ice was breaking up enough to allow us passage, and the Captain was able to force the ship down the center channel—a lot safer than near shore. Fortunately the problems we encountered were not as dangerous as those on the way north. Days became warmer, and the temperature sometimes rose to 60 degrees. I kept changing to cooler clothes.

Before going to Etah, the Commander allowed time for walrus hunting, to provide more meat for the Eskimos. They were grateful for the food and hides of the 70 animals that were killed.

As we approached Etah, on August 17th, the flags we flew told the tribe of our success. We heard shouts of welcome and saw kayaks coming out to meet us and escort us in. We were just as happy to see them. A relief ship with supplies was anchored near the *Roosevelt*. What a welcome sight! Something from home. When we were moored, our Eskimo families pushed eagerly toward the whaleboats to be the first ashore. The whole tribe waited to greet them, jumping in excitement.

The reunion of Ooqueah and his bride-to-be surprised me. Minaq came to meet us but didn't pay any special attention to her betrothed. I didn't think she was shy, just young. Probably she hardly knew him. And I had noticed that Ooqueah and other Eskimos seldom showed any emotion. I knew Ooqueah would have no rival, now, and I believed he would be kind to her.

Charley and I and the crew stayed on board. Soon we heard a welcome cry, "Mail is here!" followed by the sound of running feet. Everyone wanted to get news from home. I paced impatiently until the letters were sorted and I had mine in hand. I went to my cabin to read some from friends and Aunt Bessie, the latest dated March 23rd. She had missed me—Molly, too. Nothing unusual had happened in New York, except that she had had a ride on the new elevated train.

At dinner George asked, "Everything all right at home?"

"Yes, Aunt Bessie says a lot of people are waiting to hear about my experiences in the Arctic."

"You'll be a hero at home, now," he said, teasing me. "What's that?" he asked, pointing to a thick packet.

"Letters from some of the students at my school, and the principal. He sent his prayers for my safety. They want me to talk to them in assembly when I get home."

"They'll elect you president of the class," he said, pounding me on the back.

Maybe it wouldn't have been so bad going back there, but I had other plans now. I had no time to waste if I wanted to return to Greenland, and I believed Mr. Mac would help me prepare for that. I would go to the school and tell them about Ooqueah—how much he had taught me, and that he needed wood and tools. Maybe they could send some.

CHAPTER 24

The nights soon became dark again, and it snowed. The Commander sent meat ashore for the tribe and had 50 tons of coal reloaded for our return. He rewarded Ooqueah, Egingwah, Seegloo and Ootah with a whaleboat, gun and tent for each, and gave other faithful men and women articles priceless to them.

I promised Ooqueah, "I'm going to find a way to get back here. I'll come on a whaler or something and bring you some things you need. I love Greenland. I want to live here again for a summer so I can learn more about the glaciers and these black cliffs."

"I wait. You take Karko," he offered. "You like her. She likes you."

"Gee, Ooqueah, you're generous, but I can't. She wouldn't survive in New York—she'll be happier here. And Molly might be jealous. But I'd like you to have my football and my knife."

He gave me a wide smile, showing his white teeth, and accepted them.

"I'll miss you," I told him. "And you taught me a lot." He offered to have a final game of finger pulling. I laughed and obliged.

On the day we left, Matt hugged members of the tribe and gave them all his possessions. When we rowed out to the *Roosevelt*, men in kayaks followed us. As the ship moved slowly away, the mournful sound of the boat whistle echoed around the mountains. Matt and I stood in the stern, waving to our friends with tears in our eyes.

"I'll never see them again," Matt said.

We parted with the rest of the Eskimos at Cape York. As we steamed out of the harbor, I could feel the excitement aboard as we headed home. But Matt looked so gloomy that to cheer him I said, "You accomplished what you set out to do, Matt."

"Yes—yes, I did. It's a milestone for my race. And after 23 years in the Arctic, the Commander won the Pole for America." After a pause he said, "And you went farther than you expected, didn't you?"

"Yes, I was lucky."

"You earned it—you used all your wits and strength."

"Yeah," I agreed and laughed. "I really lived."

Out at sea I wrote this letter to mail in Labrador:

Dear Aunt Bessie:

Well, it's done! Mr. Peary reached the North Pole on April 6th, as you will probably have heard by the time this letter reaches you. I hope to be home in September and find that you and Molly are all right.

I can't wait to tell you all I have done. You'll be surprised to learn not only that I became a dog driver, but that I helped Mr. Peary on the Polar Sea. And now I understand what Father did here—I have had some unbelievable experiences.

The Eskimos are the happiest people I have ever known, and I have learned a lot from them—it's amazing to see the ways they adapt to this harsh climate. They have taught me almost as much as the assistants, who are now my friends. Mr. Mac will help me enter his school, and if he returns to the Arctic some day I hope I can go with him.

You don't need to worry about me any more. In fact, I can't wait to get started on my plans. I know now that I can do what I set out to do, and my aim is to study and become a scientist. You won't know me, Aunt Bessie. I'm bigger and a lot stronger.

I hope I may have my old room back.

Your nephew, Tom.

P.S. Wait till you hear about my sixteenth birthday.

That night I thought of Father. If only he could

have seen our victory. I wished I could tell him all about what I had done to help make his dream come true. I think he would have been proud of me. To honor his memory I resolved to continue to be strong. After all that I had survived, why should I be afraid of the future? I thought of the words of a hymn Aunt Bessie loved to sing: "Now I know what I can be, and my heart is flying free."

THE END

List of Illustrations

Bibliography

Angell, Pauline,	To the Top of the World,
	New York, Rand McNally, 1964
Astrup, Eivind,	With Peary Near the Pole,
	London, C. Arthur Pearson, Ltd., 1898
Bartlett, Robert A.,	The Log of Bob Bartlett,
	New York, Putnam, 1928
Borup, George,	A Tenderfoot with Peary,
	Fred Stokes Co., New York, 1911
Dolan, Edward F.,	Matthew Henson, Black Explorer,
	Dodd Mead, 1979
Freuchen, Peter,	Book of the Eskimos,
	Ohio, World, 1961
Green, Fitzhugh,	Peary, the Man Who Refused to Fail,
	New York and London,
	G.P. Putnam's Sons, 1926
Hayes, James Gordon,	Robert Edwin Peary: A Record of His Explorations,
	1886-1929, London, G. Richards and H. Toulin,
	1929
Henson, Matthew Alexander,	A Negro Explorer at the North Pole,
	New York, Frederick A. Stokes, 1912
Hobbs, William Herbert,	Peary, New York, MacMillan, 1936
Lord, Walter,	Peary to the Pole, New York, Harper and Row, 1963
MacMillan, Donald B.,	Etah and Beyond,
	New York, Houghton Mifflin, 1927
	How Peary Reached the Pole,
	Boston and New York, Houghton Mifflin, 1934
Miller, Floyd,	Ahdoolo: The Biography of Matthew Henson
	(1st ed.), New York, Dutton, 1963
Peary, Robert Edwin,	The North Pole,
	London, Hodder and Stoughton, 1910
	Northward Over the Great Ice (2 vols.),
	New York, Fred Stokes, 1898
	Secrets of Polar Travel, New York, Century, 1917
Robinson, Bradley,	Dark Companion (1st ed),
	New York, R.M. McBride, 1947
Weems, John E.,	Peary, the Explorer and the Man,
	Boston, Houghton Mifflin, 1967

About the Author

Barbara King, like her main character, is an adventurer who has enjoyed kayaking, sailing, white water rafting and mountain climbing. Before her retirement she was a teacher, and later a librarian in public and elementary school libraries. She has served as a docent in the Bowdoin College Peary-MacMillan Arctic Museum, where she became interested in the life of Matthew Henson and the Arctic expedition.

About the Illustrator

Mary Irwin was born in Canada, and came to the United States at the age of eight. She studied in both countries and has been an artist all her life. She was an assistant art editor for *World Book Encyclopedia*, and later taught drawing and painting to children and adults. She is listed in *Who's Who of American Women*.

Acknowledgments

The author is grateful to the following people, whose support and encouragement made this book possible:

Genevieve LeMoine, curator of the Peary-MacMillan Arctic Museum at Bowdoin College, who gave me expert advice and checked the accuracy of all information about the expedition;

Nancy Nielsen, whose generous gift of time and talent made publication possible;

Mary Irwin, who offered to do the drawings and did them so well;

Maryli Tiemann, teacher at Morse High School in Bath, Maine, who took the story to her students and gave me their reactions.

Also, my talented group of writer-friends and critic Mark Melnicove for their editorial help and encouragement, and my Maine family members – Catherine, Terry, Rachel and Brian Bell for many kinds of assistance and support.